Shadows in t
Hunt for the K

Bluthund Circle 6
Cedric Daurio

This novel is a sequel to "The Templar Quest: Shadows of the Grail". However, both books can be read independently and in any order."

This book is part of the series
Bluthund Circle.
The titles in that series are:
Runes of Fire: The Mayan Prophecy
The Gobi Codex: Lost Treasure beyond a Fleeing Horizon
Beneath the Eagle's Shadow: The Assassins Legacy
The Siberian Legacy: Hunt for the tsar's Treasure
The Templar Quest- Shadows of the Grail

The Bluthund Circle is an informal hermetic group formed on social networks. It brings together researchers from the most diverse disciplines, who collaborate in the resolution of difficult-to-manage cases. They have research methods that come from both the positive sciences and alternative knowledge, based on traditional wisdom, in arcana of different cultures.

Dramatis Personae

Nick Lafleur: French Canadian boy, 21, System analist, student of Digital Marketing.

Jiang Zhi Ruo: Chinese girl from Singapur, 20, Calligrapher and draftswoman, Tai Chi Chuan expert.

Mikhail Turgenev: Russian boy born in St Petersburg. 23, Mountain climber, student of Mechanical Engineering.

Chandice Williams: Jamaican girl, 21, classical dancer, expert in Caribbean folklore.

Jack Berglund: American, 45. Member of the Bluthund Circle, runologist, specialist in ancient alphabets.

Lakshmi Dhawan: 38, woman born in India, member of the FBI.

Anila Ragnarsson: daughter of Lakshmi and Ingo Ragnarsson, Icelandic academic.

Keneisha Sullivan: Director at the FBI, Lakshmi Boss.

Admiral B.C. Donnelly: American. Advisor to the US State Department.

Dr.W.Richardson: British, Master of the Bluthund Circle in New York.

Jerome Watkins: American, Master of Ceremonies at Bluthund events.

Madame Nadia Swarowska: Polish, Member of the Bluthund Management Committee

Suzuki Taro: Japanese, Member of the Bluthund Management Committee, expert in martial arts.

Matsuko: Young Ninja female warrior.

Corrado Gherardi, former Jesuit priest specializing in the history of religions.

Ignacio de Mendizábal (Iñaki): Bishop, leader of Divine Action.

Dr. Wolfram von Eichenberg: scholar specialized in western and eastern esotericism.

Professor Jacob Efron: Israeli archeologist.
Bertran Rostanh: Tobacconist in Carcassone.

Art Gallery

Episode 1

THE MEMBERS OF THE Bluthund Circle Assembly made their way to the meeting room that had already been set up for the second part of their session. After having made the evaluation of the previous initiative, related to the search for the Holy Grail, and a frugal lunch, they were eager to know what would be the new mission that Admiral Donnelly, Advisor to the United States Department of State would propose to them.

While everyone present took their seats, Dr. Richardson prepared some papers on the desk, and Jerome Watkins, Master of Ceremonies, prepared the projection equipment and microphones. Finally Richardson spoke.

"As I said before lunch, Admiral Donnelly will propose a new mission to us, and then the Community Executive Committee will discuss if it accepts it and if so, how we will organize the teams that will carry it out."

At that moment Watkins' cell phone rang and he took the call and then said to Donnelly. "The security guard at the reception of the building calls me. A Mrs. Ganbold and a Mr. Richart have arrived. Are they the people you are waiting for? "

The aforementioned responded immediately.

"Yes, Jerome. Please tell Louie to bring them in. " Then turning to Richardson, he added.

"They are the experts on the subject that we are going to consider. Let's wait for them to arrive before starting the meeting. "

The two new guests arrived within minutes accompanied by Louie, who immediately left. They were a man of about thirty-five, tall and thin, with reddish hair, and a woman of clear oriental origin, with a face of exotic beauty and a spectacular silhouette. Donnelly shook their hands and proceeded to introduce them to the audience.

"Special Agent Orghana Ganbold is from the Far East Section of the CIA. She is a person of Mongolian origin, born in Ulan Bator. This gentleman is Dr. Ives Richart, one of the most prestigious historians specializing in the Middle East."

Once the introductions were made, Richardson took up the floor, just to say.

"Well then, please Admiral, explain to us what is the task that the State Department proposes to the Bluthund Circle."

Donnelly stood in front of the audience and spoke briefly.

"The mission is to find the tomb of Genghis Khan."

A murmur of surprise ran through the room; the faces of the attendees clearly showed their surprise. Donnelly continued his speech.

"Although to Western minds this may seem inexplicable or unimportant, the truth is that the dilemma of the location of this tomb is in the East a mystery comparable to that represented by the Holy Grail in the West. This fact is related to the personality of this greatest warrior of the Eastern Middle Ages. The fate of his body is surrounded by as much mystery and legends as the Holy Chalice for Christians. For that reason I am going to ask three speakers to enlighten us on this subject.

"First of all I kindly ask Dr. Wolfram von Eichenberg, a member of the Bluthund Circle, to explain to us who Genghis Khan was. Forgive me Wolfram for not giving you time to prepare the subject, but I am sure that you have the necessary knowledge.

"Second, I will ask Dr. Richart to tell us about the mystery of Ghengis Khan tomb and all the failed attempts to find it. The third term I will ask Special Agent Ganbold to inform us of the reason why this tomb is a subject of high interest to the CIA. "

Donnelly took a seat and von Eichenberg stood up and took the microphone.

"Well, although the Admiral's kind invitation takes me by surprise, the life of Genghis Khan is a familiar subject, so I will try to improvise an explanation. Hope it's neat.

"Genghis Khan was the creator of the Mongol Empire, the largest in the history of mankind. In the period of his splendor this Empire occupied huge areas including most of Central Asia and China, with the Mongol invasions reaching the west to Poland, Kiev, Bulgaria and Georgia, and much of the Muslim Middle East, so he conquered much of Eurasia. Due to his military successes, he is still considered the greatest military conqueror of all time.

"Genghis Khan was born in 1158 into a noble family, and at birth he was called Temujin. He died in 1227 in dubious circumstances that have made him a legend, which I suppose the next speaker will address. After founding his empire, Temujin was proclaimed Genghis Khan, a name of Turkish origin, based on the words *tengiz sea,* which mean something like "universal sovereign".

"He based his enormous power on bringing together the nomadic tribes of Northeast Asia. His successors expanded the Empire that came to conquer or create vassal states in present-day China, Korea, the Caucasus, Central Asia, and large areas of Eastern Europe and Southwest Asia.

"Both Genghis Khan and his successors were genociders who carried out terrible massacres on the civilian populations of the conquered lands, which created them a sinister fame in the modern history of those countries.

"On the other hand, within the Mongol Empire there was an incredible expansion of science, culture and technology, which was achieved by connecting previously widely dispersed cultures with each other. Related to these achievements, we can mention the adoption of a unified Uyghur writing system for the Empire, the promotion of meritocracy and religious tolerance among peoples of very different traditions. From the point of view of communications and transport, Gengis Khan created the Silk Road under a unified political command, which brought into cultural and commercial contact huge regions of Northeast Asia, Muslim Southwest Asia and Eastern Europe, promoting progress in all those areas. Therefore, current descendants consider him the Father of Mongolia.

"About twenty thousand children are attributed to him with his more than thirty wives and innumerable concubines, so that his DNA is widely distributed in his area of influence.

"Well, friends, this is what I can tell about the life of Genghis Khan."

Richardson stood up and shaking hands with the speaker said.

"Thank you Wolfram for your excellent introduction. Next we will have a coffee-break, and then Dr. Richart will inform us about the versions related to location of the tomb of Genghis Khan."

Episode 2

Ives Richart stepped forward and took the microphone in his hands. He seemed a bit nervous, but as he began to speak his tone progressively became more confident. He spoke in English with a heavy French accent.

"The circumstances of Genghis Khan's death and burial are shrouded in the mist of mystery, and this is due above all to his will. Indeed, legend has it that he did not wish his grave site to be known later, for whatever the reasons. There are even strong versions in the sense that to keep the secret, the slaves who worked in it grave were massacred by the Khan's soldiers, and that those same soldiers were in turn exterminated, to completely seal said secret by eliminating all eyewitnesses . This shows the value of human life in the Khan's court.

"Genghis Khan died in 1227, in circumstances that as I have said are unclear. According to the Venetian traveler and merchant Marco Polo, in his book 1, chapter 50, the Khan died from a war wound when an arrow was stuck in his knee in his fight against a castle called Caaju. Other versions hold that he died of natural causes at the age of 72.

"Regarding the precautions taken by his followers to hide the place of his burial, some versions affirm that a river was diverted to cover his grave, while others maintain that the grave was trampled by numerous horses and then trees were planted on the grave. In turn, the permafrost layer that covers the suspected areas would have hidden that site, unless the widespread thaw due to global warming reveals it.

"In any case, if all the external references, such as tombstones or rocks, were removed, in the vast expanse of Mongolia it is unlikely to find such a tomb if there are no concrete references.

"If all these precautions seem excessive to us, let us remember the role of Father of Mongolia that his subjects gave him, and which is actually quite a true title, since it is estimated that 1 out of every 200 human beings alive today on the planet has part of the Khan's genes. Regarding the various versions about the burial place, we are going to cite the most widespread.

"In the first place we can cite a tradition according to which all the great Mongol chiefs and Khans must be buried in the Altäi mountains, even if they die in distant places up to a hundred days of travel from them. This is however a rather vague and imprecise location.

"Another version locates the tomb at the top of one of the Khentii Mountains, called Burkhan Khaldun, about 100 miles northeast of Ulan Bator. Apparently in his youth Gengis Khan had been hiding from his enemies in that area. "

Corrado Gherardi, Richart's old acquaintance from academia, raised a hand to ask a question.

"Tell me Corrado, do you have a question?" Said the speaker.

"Yes, Ives. I understand that in the People's Republic of China, in the Inner Mongolia area, there is a memorial mausoleum of Genghis Khan. "

"Yes it's correct. It was built between 1954 and 1956 by the Chinese government in the traditional Mongolian style. It was motivated by the worship of the Mongols to the figure of Genghis Khan, and rituals are practiced within traditional Mongolian shamanism. But it is a cenotaph, that is, an empty tomb that only contains some accessories that presumably belonged to the Khan, but there is no body. It is in Ejin Horo Qi, 115 km north of Yulin and 55 km south of Dongsheng. "

"Thanks, Ives."

The speaker continued with his lecture.

"As we have said before, one site where the tomb of the 'Universal Sovereign' has been searched is Burkhan Khaldun Mountain. Although it was previously known by another name, the current coordinates are

48.5 °N and 108.7 °E. This area has been closed to archaeologists until relatively recently. According to Yuan tradition, all the great Mongol Khans have been buried near the tomb of Genghis Khan, in a valley called Qinian. However, the location of that valley is currently unknown. "

This time it was the turn of Wolfram von Eichenberg, also an old acquaintance of Richart, to raise his hand.

"Yes, Wolfram. Do you have a question?"

"Yes. I want to know what is the attitude of the current Mongols in relation to the searches for the tomb of their hero. Are they also interested in finding it?"

Richart replied.

"I think that point will be covered at length by the next speaker, Madame Ganbold. But I can already anticipate that the Mongols are very superstitious and prefer to leave their dead alone. They have even woven legends about curses of the type that existed in the case of the tomb of another medieval conqueror, Tamerlan. "

"What are you talking about?"

"Shortly after Soviet archaeologists discovered the tomb of Tamerlane, his country was invaded by Nazi troops.

"Access to the Burkhan Khandun Mountains is restricted as it is considered to be sacred territory and both the government and the population try to keep intruders out. In addition to their desire to keep the memory of the Khan in peace, they fear the action of grave robbers, since Genghis Khan was supposed to have been buried with numerous looted treasures throughout Asia. "

This time it was Taro Suzuki who raised his hand. When the speaker gave him the floor, he said.

"I know that recently there have been attempts to locate the grave with modern methods and technologies, including by researchers associated with television channels. Did they come up with any results? "

Richart answered without hesitation.

"Indeed there has been a 'Khan Valley Project', which has used non-invasive technologies, that is, without excavating the surface of the earth. They have made a survey of all the existing aerial photos of the area and made a mosaic with them to detect suspicious sites.

"There have been ground, air and satellite searches, including drone flights for remote sensing, but the grave remains to be found."

In the absence of other questions, Dr.Richart ended his dissertation.

Dr. Richardson rose from his chair and saluting the French said.

"Thank you very much, Dr.Richart, for your clear and thorough explanation. Now we will have another coffee break, and then Madame Ganbold and Admiral Donnelly will explain to us why the discovery of the tomb of Genghis Khan is an issue that worries the United States Department of State. "

Episode 3

ORGHANA GANBOLD TOOK a few steps forward and stood in front of the audience. The male attendees admired her spectacular silhouette, wrapped in her tight pants and black leather jacket over a deep red shirt. Her exotic features were perfect; in short, she was an example of oriental beauty, and Lakshmi Dhawan, Matsuko Suzuki and Madame Nadia Swarowska looked at her with a certain envy.

Orghana spoke perfect British English but with a somewhat guttural accent and her voice was slightly husky. She spoke with the confidence of a person trained in addressing a select audience.

"I am going to start with a brief reference to my country and my people. If I make this distinction, it is to emphasize that even though I am a citizen of the People's Republic of Mongolia, all Mongols feel part of a larger historical unit, which also includes the so-called Inner Mongolia, actually the Inner Mongolia Autonomous Region, part of the People's Republic of China.

"I am going to start with a brief description of my country, the People's Republic of Mongolia. It is a gigantic nation, measuring 604,000 square miles, with only 33 million people, making it the least densely populated country in the world. It is totally surrounded by other countries and has no access to any sea, so it is totally Mediterranean. Its territory is made up of a grassy steppe, almost without any arable land. For this reason, about 30% of the population is still nomadic today, and is dedicated to raising horses.

"It is surrounded by mountains to the north and the huge Gobi Desert to the south. Its capital is Ulan Bator, or Ulaanbaatar in its modern name, and it is home to half the population. Its neighbors are the Russian Federation to the north and the Inner Mongolia Autonomous Region, part of China, to the south. It has no border with Kazakhstan for a distance of only 23 miles.

"Buddhism is the main religion and Islam the second, although it is concentrated in people of the Kazak ethnic group. The ethnic issue is of great importance to the problem that we are going to describe. 95% of the inhabitants are of Mongolian origin, and within them, the Khalka ethnic group represents 86%, and the remaining 14% of the Mongols are Oirats, Buriats and other groups. All the inhabitants speak different Mongolian dialects. The writing is done in the Russian Cyrillic alphabet.

"Minorities, including Turkish groups like the Kazaks, Tuvans and other groups are only 5% of the population, living in the western part, and include small groups of Russians, Chinese and Koreans.

"The second geographic area of importance for our issue is the already mentioned Inner Mongolia, part of China. It is also a very large area, 463,000 square miles with a population of 24 million, most of whom are predominantly Han Chinese and a minority of about five million Mongols. It is one of the most developed areas of China, and it is divided into two regions. The eastern one is ancient Manchuria, and the western one includes several large cities. The two major languages are Mandarin Chinese and Mongolian, which uses the old Mongolian writing system, unlike the one used in the Republic of Mongolia, which, as we said, is based on Russian Cyrillic.

"This long description of the geographical and ethnic aspects of the two regions that once constituted the heart of the Mongol Empire in the time of Genghis Khan and his descendants, is particularly important to understand the processes that we are going to narrate now.

The speaker took a sip of water and then continued.

"Already in the past there were other attempts to revive the glory of the Empire of the Genghis Khan, later augmented by his successor Kublai Khan by invading and conquering China and the entire Middle East. What is brewing at present is a process of great internal turmoil in the various Mongolian tribes, particularly the nomads and semi-nomads, who have not suffered an incorporation into modern life and sedentary lifestyle. These tribes, led by shamans and other extremist religious and political leaders, are seething with promises of those millennial leaders to return to the grandiose past of conquest, expelling their neighbors from the best grazing lands and sources of water for themselves and their livestock, and imposing their claims by force of arms, which are now no longer just bows and arrows, swords and spears, but rockets, automatic weapons and even modern artillery pieces supplied by radicalized Islamic groups in the Middle East, and traffickers of weapons from the dismantled arsenals of the former Soviet Union.

"This has caused alarm among neighboring countries, particularly the Russian Federation and the People's Republic of China, who recall with horror the invasions of 800 years ago, when the same scattered Mongolian and Turkish tribes united under a unified command and swept Eurasia, as it was described by the speakers who preceded me.

"Russians, in particular, fear the recurrence of revolts in the nations formerly belonging to the former Union of Soviet Socialist Republics and now independent, including Tajikistan, Uzbekistan, Kyrgyzstan, Turkmenistan, Kazakhstan and Azarbaijani. These nations, which had been forcibly incorporated to the USSR by the Soviets, have pan-Islamic and panturkish demands from time to time, which already with the fall of the USSR produced bloody wars in Chechnya and other areas of Central Asia.

"In particular, Russians fear instability in the Mongolian People's Republic, my country, actually a satellite country of Moscow. Kyrgyzstan, the only democratic country in the entire region, is viewed with concern by the whole world.

"What everyone is fearing is that behind the search for the tomb of Genghis Khan by unidentified groups, to which the next speaker will refer, the germ of widespread rebellion of the Mongolian and Turkish peoples may be hidden.

"Well, this is what I had prepared to tell you today. If you have any questions I will answer them to the best of my ability. "

In the face of the general silence, Dr. Richardson stood up and spoke.

"Thank you, Orghana, for your magnificent explanation of the entire process that is unfolding in Central East Asia. As usual in our meetings, now we are going to have another coffee break to stretch our legs. Next, Admiral Donnelly will explain what the United States Department of State is concerned with in relation to all this problem and will make his work proposal to the Bluthund Circle. "

Episode 4

Admiral Donnelly began his speech as Jerome Watkins projected aerial images showing a caravan of typical Mongolian wagons loaded with people and various objects, escorted by horsemen mounted on spirited horses wandering through the grassy steppe, all of them followed by herded cattle lead by other younger riders.

"This image, which seems to be taken from a 13th century engraving, was nevertheless taken a few days ago with a drone, in the north of the Republic of Mongolia. What it is showing is a tribe on its march to a place that we do not know, and that is repeated by dozens in the Asian steppe. It is a nation in movement, and according to our analysts, it is not just a matter of seasonal migrations following sites with abundant pastures.

"This photograph graphically summarizes what Orghana Ganbold has just narrated, and explains our fears, which in this case are shared by the government of the Republic of Mongolia itself, and especially by its neighbors in the Russian Federation, the People's Republic of China and the government of Kazakhstan.

"All these actors of the reality of the Far East are terrified by the possibility of a massive uprising of the nomadic tribes of Outer and Inner Mongolia, accompanied by other tribes of Turkish, Muslim or shamanic ethnic groups, who feel they have the ability to change the entire world, just as they did eight centuries ago.

"We know that behind these movements are Muslim agitators, many of them Shiites, but not all. These agitators are actually terrorists who have kept the Middle East ablaze for decades, and who have access to modern weapons, as already explained coming from dismantled

Soviet arsenals, as well as artifacts made by themselves. We do not rule out that certain millennial sects in Japan and Korea join this panorama.

"What we fear above all is the appearance of a messianic leader, who can emerge in the midst of this social environment, and who can guide this hitherto inorganic movement, in a true crusade against the civilized world. The worst thing is that we believe that the emergence of that leader is only a matter of time.

"Analysts think that in order to gain credibility with the nomadic masses, these leaders must raise a flag that is meaningful to all tribesmen. We believe that the finding of the tomb of Genghis Khan may be that flag, and we tremble at what may happen if one of those leaders can claim to be the reincarnation of the Great Khan. "

At that point Dr. Richardson raised his hand.

"Yes, Dr. Richardson, do you have a question?" Said Donnelly.

"Yes. From what I understand, in this case, unlike the search for the Holy Grail or others in which we have participated before, what the State Department wants is not to find said tomb, but on the contrary that it never appears. "

"Dr. Richardson, that's an essential point. I will respond to you as best I can under the current circumstances. What we really want is for the terrorists not to find it, but that is beyond our reach, as it depends on the luck factor. What we really want is that if the tomb of the Universal Sovereign is found, we will find it and not the agitators. This would humiliate them and leave them flagless in front of the nomadic masses. "

The one who then raised his hand was Taro Suzuki. When the Admiral invited him to speak, the Japanese professor asked.

"Have you found any of those leaders so far who can become head of the tribes movement?" "So far we have not detected it, but we firmly believe that ten, twenty, one hundred candidates should be preparing in the entire steppe to lead the tribes."

Donnelly's statement shocked the participants, communicating the potential gravity of the issue and the urgency of taking action.

The dissertation lasted little longer, and at its conclusion it was time for questions from the members of the Bluthund Circle. Richardson asked a question that was on everyone's mind.

"What is the role that the State Department hopes our Community can play in this complicated matter?"

Donnelly evidently expected this question, so he answered immediately.

"Two issues. First do your own research on the possible locations of the Great Khan's tomb and communicate them to our people. Second, detect if any of the potential candidates to lead this uprising takes primacy over others, and also give us their data. "

Then Jack Berglund asked.

"What would you do with the tip we pass you on about a dangerous leader."

"What all governments do in that case."

"Namely?"

"Neutralize him."

Again, the harshness of the Admiral's words produced a murmur through the room. Nadia Swarowska whispered in Richardson's ear, who was sitting next to her.

"That is to say that we would be passing a capital sentence on the man we indicate."

Instead of answering Richardson stood up and said.

"The Department of State of the United States Government has proposed to our Community a very precise order. The next step is to immediately hold a meeting of the Executive Committee of the Community to accept or decline the assignment. We will do it immediately, while the rest of the attendees can remain in the room to await the verdict. "

Then Richardson, accompanied by Madame Swarowska, Taro Suzuki, Jack Berglund, Jerome Watkins, and von Eichenberg, retired to the former's office to discuss.

The meeting lasted over an hour, due to the importance of the subject and the material and moral implications of Bluthund's participation. Finally the members of the Executive Committee joined the other members in the large room, and Richardson, in his capacity, said.

"The Bluthund Circle has decided to accept the challenge trusted to it by the State Department. The group that will be in charge of the investigation will be made up of Jack Berglund, Taro Suzuki, Orghana Gambold and Ives Richard, and will have Jerome Watkins as support and contact in New York, if they all accept the mission. "

Episode 5

The travelers took the Turkish Airlines flight from JFK Airport in New York City to Ginggis Khaan Airport in Ulan Bator, with a total flight time of almost twenty hours. When they finally arrived in the capital of the Republic of Mongolia it was night, and it was difficult for them to get a means of transport from the airport to the hotel in the city, where they already had reservations.

Although they had been served a light dinner on the plane, they decided to eat something in a cafeteria that was open all night waiting for passengers. The topic of conversation, predictably, was the flight alternatives and the first impression that the city of Ulan Bator had made on them.

The next morning, after breakfast, Jack received a call on his cell phone. The others stepped aside to give him privacy.

"Hello... where are you? In Ulan Bator? I thought you were coming later ... Yes of course I want to see you ... Where? ... Well, I'll find out where it is or I'll look it up on Google Maps. I'm out now. "

After cutting off the call, talking to the others, Jack told them.

"I am going to meet someone I know. I'll be back at noon. I'm going to rent a car for our activities. "

If the others were surprised to learn that Berglund had acquaintances in Mongolia, they hid it, and Taro Suzuki hid a fatherly smile.

By midmorning Orghana communicated to Taro and Ives.

"I'm going to call an old acquaintance who will be our local contact. As you know, I was born in Ulan Bator and my family is from this city. "

29

"Who is that acquaintance?" Taro asked.

"His given name is Khulan , and he is a member of the Mongolian Army Intelligence services."

"It seems that he can prove valuable. Do you think he can be trusted?"

"He is a personal friend of my family. He has held me in his arms when I was born. I have absolute confidence in him."

After making a call, Orghana returned and informed her companions. "We are going to meet for dinner at a restaurant I know 7 p.m. Khulan knows the owner and will get a private room on the top floor,"

"Well, by that time Jack will be back." Said Taro.

"He said he would be back at noon." replied Ives.

Taro smiled again and said.

"I don't think he'll be back at noon."

Jack Berglund parked the truck he had rented, a worn but robust Toyota Tacoma with a full body, but he was careful to leave it two blocks from where he was going. Then he walked on foot until he reached the door of a discreet hotel, which only had a small bronze sign written in the Cyrillic alphabet and in Chinese.

As he entered he saw the janitor reading a yellowed newspaper in the dim light of a lamp, while a cigarette dangled from his lip

Jack asked in English.

"The young Japanese woman?"

"Room 5, down the hall."

Upon arriving in front of the room, the American knocked on the door with his knuckles, and a female voice from within answered him.

"Come in Jack. It is open."

As he did so, and once his eyes adjusted to the semi-darkness of the room, he made out a wide bed in which was a young oriental woman with a small body and very light skin, completely naked.

"Get undressed and come with me." Said the woman.

When Berglund returned to the hotel, his colleagues did not comment. Orghana just told him.

"We have an appointment at 7 p.m. with an old contact of mine, a member of the Mongolian army. "

The meeting place was a fairly luxurious typical Mongolian restaurant. The owner attended them personally upon entering and after a brief dialogue in Mongolian with Orghana he escorted them to the upper floor, which was divided into two large rooms. One of them was illuminated and upon entering they saw a man in his sixties, dressed in European clothes, who, upon seeing them arrive, rushed to meet Orghana, speaking briefly with her in Mongolian, until their eyes filled with tears. Then the woman said to her comrades.

"Excuse this intimate scene, but Colonel Khulan is a friend of my family and I have known him since I was a child. He speaks perfect English because he has been as a military *attaché* in various embassies of the Republic of Mongolia, so we will continue in that language. "

The first part of the meeting was of a general nature, and the Colonel outlined the political and social situation in his country. Orghana deftly guided the conversation to the topic that interested them. Khulan was evidently aware of the lady´s role in the US CIA, so the issue was not explicitly mentioned.

"In all neighboring countries of Mongolia there is a lot of concern with the millennial movement that is brewing, and it is feared that one or more leaders will emerge who may vindicate the figure of Genghis Khan, considered by all Mongols as the father of the Nation, and lead a widespread uprising of nomadic Mongols and other related tribes that can spark a wave of very violent conflict. We know that there is an influx of very modern weapons from ex-Soviet arsenals, and the old rifles that the tribesmen had are being replaced by the latest Kalashnikov models. We are aware that instructors in the use of these weapons have been brought in from Muslim governments and terrorist movements and that there are shooting ranges not too far from Ulan Bator. " Confessed Khulan.

"Why does the Mongolian government not act to curb these activities that concern them?" Asked Taro Suzuki.

"There are many internal struggles in the government, and there are sectors that sympathize with the rebel cause, which causes an immobilization of the State and its institutions, including the Army to which I belong."

"What about the governments of neighboring countries?" Inquired Jack Berglund.

"The Russian Federation is terrified by the possibility that Turkic tribes and other ethnic groups that inhabit its enormous Siberian territory could be infected. The People's Republic of China is also concerned that the movement is spreading to the Inner Mongolia Autonomous Region, part of China. And Kazakhstan knows that in its country there are tribal groups that want to form a great pan-Mongolian and pan-Turkic nation. "

"What do you think is missing for a great outbreak to emerge throughout the region?"

"We believe that the situation could quickly become complicated if a leader emerges to impose his will on the main tribes. Once this happens, the subordination of the other ethnic groups will continue like wildfire. "

Episode 6

Before Khulan's statement, the travelers had their assumptions confirmed. For the first time, Orghana spoke to the Colonel in English.

"Tell me Khulan, have you detected any tribal chief who could stand out above the rest and become that much feared Genghis Khan risen?"

The Mongol thought for a moment before answering.

"Yes, Princess, there is a tribal chief named Baatar, who has managed to gather about five major tribes behind his name. He has eliminated a couple of opponents by simply fighting in the traditional way with them and cutting their throats. A very violent man. "

Khulan's statement shocked travelers for two reasons. In the first place the confirmation of a potential enemy in full development of his plan, and secondly the title of princess attributed to Orghana. Jack looked at Taro in the eye and the Japanese made him a sly sign suggesting that he not comment at the moment.

The woman spoke to her companions and indicated.

"You should know that Baatar, in addition to a surname, is a nickname that means Hero. A very convenient nickname for a presumed successor to Genghis Khan. "

She then turned to Khulan again and asked

"In what geographical area does this Baatar move?"

"We have very diffuse information, and their tribes are nomadic and constantly on the move. In general we have located him in the area of the Tarvagatai Mountains, about 550 kilometers west of Ulan Bator, or about 350 miles. It is a wild area, completely depopulated, with the exception of wandering tribes in search of pasture for their cattle. "

Jack looked on Google Maps and after a few minutes he said.

" That area of mountains is centered on the coordinates 48.068460 N and 98.3180055 E. That gives us a clue to begin the search."

"Are you thinking of going alone? It sounds like a very dangerous idea to me? I will not let you go alone. I will accompany you and have an extraction process ready for the area if the situation gets complicated? "

"Extraction?" Ives asked puzzled.

"A helicopter rescue, if necessary." Khulan replied.

"You are a member of the Mongolian army. You can't get involved. " Orghana replied.

"Princess, what I cannot do is let you and your camrades take such a great risk without my involvement, no matter the consequences. It is the least I can do for your father, to whom I owe everything I am and what I have. "

The forceful phrase ended the discussion. The rest of the conversation referred to the preparations for the expedition, which was set for three days later, in order to give the travelers time to prepare the necessary items, including fuel, tents and sleeping bags, food and maps.

"Don't worry about the weapons, I'll take care of the necessary ones." Said Khulan. Upon returning to the hotel, Jack Berglund and Taro Suzuki were left alone in the cafeteria to talk while the others went to their rooms.

"All our suspicions are confirmed, and I think this contact will lead us to at least one specific clue." Jack expressed. Instead of answering, Taro leaned back in his chair, and staring at his companion, he said.

"I suppose you have noticed the treatment the colonel has given Orghana."

"You obviously mean the fact that he has called her Princess."

"Yes."

"You know oriental customs better than I do. Do you think it was just a polite way of speaking, or did it reflect something real? "

"No one would give a royal treatment if it had no basis in reality." Taro thought for a moment and added.

"The truth is that we don't really know who Orghana Ganbold is, if she is simply a CIA special agent, or if she has some other interest in Mongolian affairs."

"Another issue, have you seen how Ives Richart looks at her?"

"I'm not a good observer of these things." Replied Jack.

"In a small group like ours, it is necessary to take into account all the factors that may have an impact on the results. The man seems bewitched by her. "

"She is a very beautiful woman, a true oriental beauty. You know that Caucasian men are often attracted to that kind of woman."

"Including you." Stated Taro with a smile.

" It's true."

They got up early in the morning. They had used the previous two days to buy supplies, fuel, tents, sleeping bags and blankets, to be able to spend the hard Siberian nights in the open air, especially when they were at a certain height.

The group left the hotel and drove fifteen kilometers to the west (about ten miles). Ives was driving, as he proved to be an excellent rural and mountain driver. At one point, Jack, who was in the passenger seat, pointed to a cabin on the side of the road.

"That must be the house where Khulan is waiting for us." He said.

Indeed, when parking next to the house, the Colonel left the dilapidated house, which was obviously abandoned; he was dragging a couple of boxes.

"Those boxes must contain the weapons he told us about." Expressed Orghana. "It seems to include some long weapons."

Taro meditated and asked the girl.

"Are you familiar with firearms?"

"Of course."

The answer sounded excessively forceful, so that the woman felt compelled to moderate it emphasis a bit.

"I mean, the CIA training ... you know."

"Of course." The Japanese's face was inscrutable.

Jack and Khulan loaded the boxes into the vehicle, everyone got into it, and Ives started driving again. Inside the truck, Khulan opened the boxes and extracted the contents, which then passed from hand to hand. Orghana, Jack and Khulan himself inspected the two AK 47 assault rifles and the five Makarov 9mm pistols, noting that they were in good condition and clean. The supply of ammunition was also abundant.

With his usual contempt for firearms, Taro commented sarcastically.

"There is enough for a little war."

"It is not only the alleged supporters of Genghis Khan who can assault us. There are highway robbers and caravan raiders in the desert. " Khulan replied firmly.

"There is no other man in the Republic of Mongolia who is as familiar with the security situation in the country as Colonel Khulan." Added Orghana.

The small villages followed one another: Lun, Bayannuur, Avdzaga. Changes of course and directions were frequent, and as the kilometers lagged behind, boredom invaded the travelers. After about 250 kilometers (160 miles) they turned northwest, and upon reaching Khushuut they stopped.

There they ate a light snack. Khulan consulted with some villagers about the state of the road going forward and the weather conditions, while Orghana paid attention. When she returned with his companions, Jack asked her.

"What are they saying?"

"The problems start here. The road becomes rougher and there is a storm brewing. "

With that daunting prospect, they decided to keep going, while Jack replaced Ives at the wheel. Khulan would do the final driver, because of his familiarity with the landscape. Meanwhile, the sky was turning dark.

Episode 7

From Khushuut they decided to take a path that went southwest, passing through Jargalant until it joined another road that headed northwest. The panorama was the usual Mongolian steppe of hard grasses and the travelers dozed from time to time, while the three drivers of the vehicle alternated to avoid that the monotony of the landscape produced a hypnotic effect and took away their reflexes.

They left the village named Tsertserleg behind, and the soft green hills gave way to the desert devoid of vegetation. When they passed Zaankhushuu, the map only showed them a desert area ahead. Ives was driving again, and Khulan was riding in the passenger seat. At one point Orghana, who was sitting in the second row of seats, touched the Colonel's shoulder, indicating a dark line on the horizon.

Khulan replied with concern.

"Yes, princess. I've already seen it ten minutes ago. "

"What happen?" Asked Jack Berglund. "What is that line?"

"It's a dust storm." Replied the Mongolian. "What direction does it lead?"

"It is approaching us with speed."

"Does it represent a danger?" inquired Ives.

"Very big. There are stories of entire caravans that are buried by these moving land masses. " Orghana's tone was alarmed.

"Can we find some shelter?"

"Impossible. This is a completely flat area, without forests or mountains. "

"Can't we go back?"

"We would never be on time. These storms travel at speeds much greater than that of our vehicle. We only can pray. " Was Khulan's tremendous conclusion.

Dust storms typically originate in the Gobi Desert, located in northwest China and southwest of the Republic of Mongolia. They travel great distances before disappearing into the atmosphere, and the location of the travelers was in the range of these phenomena. They are quite unpredictable, since although the most frequent occur in March and April, they still exist in months as far apart as October and November.

Travelers know the fearsome signals consisting of a kind of cigar-shaped cloud that occurs on the horizon, in this case from the south. They advance at great speed, covering not only caravans and travelers but towns, cities and crops, ruining the respiratory health of the population, spoiling their crops, killing livestock and burying countless travelers on their way.

Little by little the atmosphere around the truck changed. The air was becoming electrified by the rubbing of the innumerable dust particles with the molecules of the air and with each other.

The vision in front of them was also undergoing great changes. Indeed, what had previously been a simple outline on the horizon was already acquiring relief and thickness and was clearly distinguished as a light brown cloud with darker streaks.

The first particles of sand, ahead of the storm, began to hit the windshield of the vehicle, and the atmosphere in front of them became less clear. The travelers had their eyes fixed on the ominous stain that grew by leaps and bounds. In the vehicle that was transporting them, Orghana, sitting in the seat next to the drivers, looked straight ahead at the cloud, watching it gain height as it approached, blocking the dark sky.

In a couple of minutes the gigantic brown cloud was over them and engulfed the truck, so that the passengers lost sight of the stretch of steppe that stretched out in front of them, and within seconds they did not even see the engine cover of the truck in which they were traveling. Visibility dropped to zero and what had been a loud whistle of the wind was transformed into a deafening roar. Rocked by the blizzard, the car lurched to both sides threatening to overturn. Finally the monstrous cloud covered completely the entire landscape, the engine stopped working due to the contamination that covered the carburetor and the injection pumps.

A gust of wind took the truck sideways, skidded it, lifted it onto her sinister bosom, and spun it. Nature piously unplugged the brains of the vehicle crew while outside the elements were unleashed furiously amid the gloomy roar of the wind.

Orghana felt someone shake her right arm vigorously. She half-opened her eyes, which fortunately had been protected from the dust by the goggles, but when she tried to breathe her airways clogged and she involuntarily coughed to clear them. Her mouth was also full of sand and she spat in order to speak. Only then did she realize that Ives was the one who had woken her up from her swoon. The woman smiled weakly at him; she had already noticed the fortitude and courage of the French when she watched him drive in the midst of the turmoil of the storm, before they both lost consciousness; a feeling of admiration for the man had grown inside her.

"Come help me with the other three."Said Ives. At that moment the Mongol took charge of the situation around her. The truck in which they were traveling, after turning several times on itself driven by the wind, had remained on its four wheels although the interior was a chaos of packages and belongings. Orghana looked out in fear due to her recent memory and was surprised to see a clear sky after the storm. Looking around, she saw that Jack, Taro, and Khulan were awkwardly moving across the ground, brushing the dust off their faces, their hands, and their clothes. Jack and Khulan were clearly disoriented.

She unfastened her seat belt and, with difficulty opening the door on her side due to the accumulated sand in front of her, she got out of the truck and helped Taro to succor the other two; the woman sighed with relief when she noted that both men were breathing and moving, although Jack was streaming blood from his forehead from a blow probably produced by some object in the rollover.

"Hope I find the first aid kit in the middle of all this morass." said Taro addressing his friend. "Luckily you don't need stitches."

The Japanese then turned to Ives and told him.

"Did you want to come to the East for adventures? Well, you can't complain. "

The Frenchman smiled weakly, still not convinced that he had not suffered any injuries in the tremendous overturning of the vehicle.

Jack also came over to check the status of his companions.

"We cannot complain. The van and those of us who were traveling in it are relatively well. There will be a few chores to do to get the engine running again. The problem is to find again the path that we had been following. It is not in sight, it simply disappeared from the landscape. "

Episode 8

As soon as they got the car engine working, they returned to the last town they had been to, called Zaankhushuu, to replenish supplies that had been lost in the rollover and as a result of the dust; this included water, food and fuel. The village, too, had been hit by the dust storm and its few inhabitants were reclaiming their scattered possessions, herding their livestock and cleaning their houses.

After a kind negotiation, they reached an agreement with a local family to be able to use the modest facilities of the house and wash themselves, heal their wounds and sleep indoors.

The next day they had breakfast with the host family, whose members only spoke a Mongolian dialect, with whom Orghana and Khulan discussed the difficulties of the journey ahead. They claimed to be archaeologists looking for signs of traditional culture, which was partially true, and were told that there were no ruins in the area of ancient populations, which was predictable due to the nomadic character of the tribes in the area, especially in the past.

One of the daughters of the family, a young and pretty maiden, was looking insistently at Ives Richart, which made Orghana nervous, since was exploring her own feelings for the Frenchman: Taro, who did not lose detail of the reactions of the people around him, looked at the scene of jealousy with amusement.

Khulan was leading the talk to the issues that really interested them, and revealed the feeling of pride that the image of Genghis Khan awakened in these simple people.

When he tried to inquire about the presence of presumed heirs of the Great Khan, the Colonel found elusive answers from the locals, so he preferred not to delve into the subject so as not to raise alarms among the followers of the presumed leader named Bataar.

At one point, the head of the host family said, after meditation.

"You must be careful with the bandits that ravage this region."

"What are you referring to?" asked Khulan.

"Assailants of caravans and travelers. They steal horses and camels, destroy cars, take weapons and food and even water, and kill the victims, or leave them to starve and die of thirst in the desert. Very cruel people. Every so often corpses of the victims appear, destroyed by vultures. "

A chill ran through the bodies of Orghana, Ives, and Jack. The patriarch continued.

"You should avoid stopping anywhere along the way, because they might be ambushed even under the ground. You should be cautious if you see signs on the horizon, which may be of men on horseback on the march. "

Jack gave a reward in Mongolian money to the gentle hosts for their hospitality. Then the travelers dusted the interior and exterior of the van, loaded their belongings, and set off again on the dubious road that led to the Tarvagatai Mountains, in their search for the heir to Genghis Khan.

When they were leaving Taro received one of the mysterious calls on his satellite phone, and spoke a few words in Japanese, but did not comment on it.

Shortly after, Jack saw flashes on a hill higher than the rest of the landscape, undoubtedly produced by the sun on some reflective surface. He indicated the site to Taro, who was sitting next to him. The Japanese told him.

"Don't worry, there is no danger."

Knowing his friend, Berglund associated that response with the call previously received by the martial arts teacher.

After a couple of hours of driving, they spotted on the right side of the road a tiny village, which according to the Google map, was called Teel, located on gentle hills and by a medium-sized lagoon.

As it was getting dark they decided to spend the night in the next town, called Tariat Xopro, larger than the previous one, and which according to the maps had a hotel and a guest house. The travelers needed to be able to shower, change clothes, have some dirty clothes washed, eat decently, and sleep in a clean bed before continuing on their journey.

Once they arrived in town and checked in the hotel. Jack contacted Dr. Richardson of the Bluthund Circle in New York City. In that mmento, his companions left him alone so that he could speak in a reserved way. When the call ended, Jack joined the others.

"You have news?" Asked Taro Suzuki.

"Yes, I explained to Richardson where we are and he asked me to stay here for a couple of days, awaiting the arrival of Aman Bodniev, whom you know."

Addressing the other three comrades he added.

"Aman is a Siberian shaman, who has already participated in numerous adventures with us, and has saved our lives more than once."

"But is he in Russia or in Mongolia?" asked Ives.

"Aman permanently wanders throughout Northeast Asia, he appears in the most unlikely places."

The day was generally of rest, since the city did not offer points of interest. Going down to breakfast the next day, Ives found himself looking out the cafeteria window out into the street and at one point expressed some apprehension.

"Look at that character who is standing in front of the hotel door. He is truly awesome. "

As he leaned out, Jack exclaimed loudly, with a festive tone.

"That is Aman Bodniev. Look Taro, he is our friend. "

After looking out the window and not answering, the Japanese left through the hotel door, followed by Berglund, and after running across the street, they hugged the man outside. He was a giant about two meters tall, very robust, about sixty years old, dressed in a fur coat and a Siberian hat of the same material, which made him look like a polar bear. Finally Jack dragged him to the hotel, where Orghana, Ives Richart, and Khulan were waiting at the lobby.

Jack was in charge of the introductions and together they improvised an explanation of the reason for their presence in the Republic of Mongolia. Bodniev replied in his rudimentary English.

"Dr. Richardson explained to me briefly but I had not fully understood what is the reason to reopen an issue that has been closed for seven centuries, and can ignite violent feelings."

They stayed until lunchtime exchanging experiences, and then Jack himself said.

"Okay, now we can load the truck and head out for the final leg of our search."

Episode 9

From Tariat Xopro the trail headed west, with some oscillations due to orographic reasons. According to the map, the distance to the beginning of the Tarvagatai Mountains was about 50 kilometers, and the landscape became progressively more mountainous. For that reason, the travelers doubled their precautions, since the rocky landscape allowed the presence of eventual assailants ambushed behind cliffs and in deep spells. While Ives drove the truck and Jack acted as navigator, in the two rows of rear seats the other four travelers were constantly watching the sides of the road, the low mountain peaks that were appearing, and the path that they left behind. On their knees they carried their weapons ready to face possible surprise actions. Khulan was squinting at the scene with high-powered military binoculars, and so he was the first to spot the first disturbing sign.

"There! On that high hill that is behind these other closer ones. " He said suddenly.

"What do you see?" Asked Orghana .

The colonel handed her the binoculars.

"I see three static points on the top of the hill." Said the woman.

"They are three Mongol horsemen." Replied the military man.

"That's right. Now they are disappearing behind the hill. They have no doubt realized that we discovered them. " Added the woman.

"Hiding makes them doubly suspicious." Said Bodniev. "I don't think they are alone."

"These are undoubtedly explorers controlling access to the mountains from the populated centers to the east of the mountains."

"The only question is whether they are highway robbers or something else." Added Suzuki.

"What do you mean?" Inquired Orghana.

"They can also be sentinels for the presumed heir of Genghis Khan, the leader they call Baatar."

"Two disturbing alternatives." Ives said as he steered the vehicle.

"But that we have to be prepared to face, since we are entering their territory." concluded Bodniev.

As winter was advancing, night fell earlier. They parked the truck taking advantage of the shelter of some tall rocks that emerged solitary on the terrain of the steppe, part of the first foothills of the Tarvagatai Mountains. In this way they took cover from the cold night wind that was already beginning to blow, and also prevented hostile eyes from detecting their position, particularly when they lit a fire to heat their food, warm the tents and drive away wild animals.

Bodniev and Orghana prepared dinner, and after finishing, the Russian produced a bottle of vodka from under his clothes, which he circulated to the group.

"To fight the cold from within." He expressed.

As it was still early, they began a chat around the fire, which would allow them to get to know each other a little better. The shaman recounted experiences from his extensive travels through the Russian taiga, and Jack recounted what happened with the recent expedition in search of the Holy Grail, which had begun in Argentine Patagonia and ended in the Siberian taiga.

Taro Suzuki was observing the dynamics of the scene without participating in the conversation, and once he judged that there was already enough camaraderie and trust between the members of the group, who came from very diverse origins, he interposed a decisive question.

"Orghana, I think it's time you told us who you are."

By the unexpected, the phrase produced a prolonged silence in the conversation. The woman seemed a bit confused and she managed to answer.

"You know, Admiral Donnelly introduced me, I work at the CIA and ..."

Even at the risk of appearing unkind, Suzuki interrupted her and asked again.

"No, dear girl, that is the version that was presented to us on the first day, but now I ask you who you *really* are." Taro emphasized the word "really".

Jack and Ives Richart settled on the floor. Obviously, everyone was interested in the answer to the question of the Japanese, who was known for his sagacity.

When Orghana raised her head and looked at them, something had changed in her, an intense glow was emerging from her eyes and everyone noticed the change. The woman made a sign with her head; she nodded at Khulan, as if authorizing him to speak. The Mongol colonel slowly began the narration.

"When the October Revolution occurred in Russia, back in 1917, great struggles developed throughout Asia, between the Bolsheviks and the counterrevolutionaries called Whites.

"In Mongolia a king named Bogd Khan ruled, but then was expelled by the Chinese, who put a puppet in his place. A Russian military supporter of the monarchy, Baron von Ungern Sternberg, placed at his command a formidable army of Mongol warriors, nomadic troops with great mobility and firepower, who, under Ungern's expert military leadership, drove the Chinese from power and reinstated who Mongols considered to be their rightful king, Bogd Khan.

BARON UNGERN'S REAL purpose was to reestablish the Empire also in Russia and put a Grand Duke on the throne of his country. He was finally defeated and shot by the Russians. In Mongolia the king remained for a time, after having promised the people to reestablish the Mongol Empire of Genghis Khan, of whom he was a direct descendant. "

"In what form is Orghana related to that episode?" Jack asked somewhat impatiently. Taro made a disguised sign to slow down his momentum, while Khulan began the narration again.

"Orghana is actually the daughter of a head of a mighty Mongol tribe, which makes her also a descendant of King Bogd Khan. But there is more genealogical data. "

"What are you referring to?" Ives Richart insisted, obviously interested in everything related to the lady.

"Bogd Khan was a direct descendant of Genghis Khan. That is the reason why all the tribes were subordinate to him. "

"That also makes Orghana a descendant of Genghis Khan." concluded The French.

Khulan continued speaking.

"That's right. That is her parental descent. But her ancestry through her mother's way is also interesting. "

Everyone was already absorbed listening to the words of the Colonel, who continued.

"Orghana's older sister, named Tsegseg, is the highest priestess of Tengrism." At that point it was Bodniev who interrupted, since the subject was his direct concern.

"Tengrism is the shamanic and animistic religion of Mongolia. It is a rite that mixes traditional Asian shamanism with Buddhism. "

"That is the yellow Tengrism." explained Khulan. "But Orghana's mother belongs to the branch of Black Tengrism, the true original religion of the Mongolian people."

At that moment Bodniev could not suppress an exclamation. Jack looked at his friend in surprise and asked.

"Well, Aman, please share with us what you know on this topic."

Episode 10

S itting on the ground, Aman Bodniev leaned back and narrowed his eyes. Addressing Orghana he said.

"To begin with, I met your sister Tsegseg a few years ago, when we were on the trail of the King of Mongolia's treasure, hidden by Baron von Sternberg and his men from his enemies. Do you remember her? " He added referring now to Taro and Jack.

"Of course I remember Tsegseg, an unforgettable character." replied Jack Berglund, while Suzuki nodded. The shaman continued his narration.

"When her mother decided to retire because of her age, Tsegseg took her place as High Priestess of Black Tengrism. I didn't know she had a younger sister. "

He added referring to Orghana; once again Khulan answered for the lady.

"Orghana was a little girl, and her parents had sent her first to Europe and then to the United States, to save her from persecution by the Bolsheviks. Unlike today, it was a very turbulent time. "

"What can you tell us about Black Tengrism in particular Asked Ives Richart, always interested in everything concerning Orghana.

Aman continued.

"It is an ancient ritual, dating from before the time of the Great Khans. It had an important role precisely in the time of Genghis Khan, in whose court it was a usual practice. We must not forget that his subjects attributed a divine origin to the Great Khan; he was an incarnation of the gods on Earth. On the other hand, we have already said that the Great Khan practiced religious tolerance in his court. "

Khulan nodded, while Orghana listened with her eyes fixed on the horizon, seemingly in a trance. Bodniev went on.

"Black Tengrism is related to magic, unlike Yellow Tengrism, which is a traditional religion, but nothing more."

Ives's face showed disbelief, in a low voice he muttered.

"Is there a dose of superstition in that belief?"

Aman answered.

"Your western training causes you that prejudice, but we...I mean Jack Berglund, Taro Suzuki and me, we have seen things that have no explanation in that mentality."

"Things like what?" insisted the Frenchman.

"PRINCESS TSEGSEG HAS inherited the powers of her ancestors. The tradition is that the *Ugdans*, that is, the priestesses, transmit these powers to their older daughters. "

"Including magical powers?" Ives insisted

"Yes, as well as the possibility of going into hypnotic trances and having visions of the future."

"Have you witnessed those magical powers?" This time, Richart's question was directed at Taro and Jack. The latter also leaned back slightly in a position of remembrance. His voice was deep.

"We have seen Tsegseg walk up the slopes of the mountain and surprise her enemies from behind, violating the law of gravity... I remember her transfiguration on the gold bullion-covered altar of the King of Mongolia's treasury. "

Suzuki nodded his head making a guttural sound. Jack added, addressing the Frenchman.

"I'm sorry if this conflicts with your beliefs, Ives, but it's what we've seen."

At that moment Khulan entered the conversation.

"There is only one point where I disagree with Shaman Bodniev's narrative."

"What is it about?"

"The *ugdan*, meaning the acting High Priestess, can not only transmit her powers to her eldest daughter, but to all women who are related to her by blood ties."

"I didn't know that." Admitted Aman.

"Is it to say that her mother may have passed her powers on to Orghana as well?" Ives inquired with a strange fervor.

"This is not just a supernatural transmission of energy, but a long training." replied the Colonel.

"Training in what disciplines?"

"Martial arts, natural medicine, deception and mass hypnosis."

"Collective hypnosis? Do you mean that what we have witnessed, Tsegseg literally walking by the side of the hill ... it happened only in our mind? " Asked Jack.

"We don't know if it happened in reality or only in our perceptions." The Russian replied with his deep voice.

Taro Suzuki decided to add information from his experience to Khulan's response.

"As an oriental martial arts instructor, I am certainly aware of the Mongol priestesses' warrior teaching tradition passed down to their female students."

Suddenly Ives stood in front of the fire, took two steps towards Orghana and asked.

"Have you been trained by your mother and sister in the arts of Black Tengrism, and have they passed their powers to you?"

Orghana stood up too and took a step toward Ives Richart. She stared into his eyes for a long time, in which she was obviously penetrating into the Frenchman's mind and soul. Once she had made the desired conclusion, guttural sounds came from her lips in a language unknown to others.

Richart dropped to one knee and looked down at the ground. The woman placed her left hand on his head and then uttered another sentence equally incomprehensible to others.

Even the slight night breeze calmed down, as if associating itself with the intensity of the moment.

Without saying a word, Orghana took Richart by the arm, pulled him to his feet, and led him toward her tent, behind whose cloth door they disappeared. Khulan also left for his own tent.

Only Jack Berglund, Taro Suzuki and Aman Bodniev remained around the fire. The American looked puzzled.

Addressing the shaman he asked his friend.

"Aman, I am completely confused. I think you understood better than I did what happened at the end of the conversation, and perhaps you even understood what Orghana said to Ives. Could you please explain to us? "

"Dear friend. My conclusion is that no one on this mission in Mongolia is what he claims to be. The language in which Orghana spoke is a forgotten language now known only to the high priests and seers who direct the greatest magical traditions of East and West. I am a simple shaman from the Siberian taiga. I did not understand everything that Princess Orghana said; but I have noticed that she recognized Ives Richart as an adept to the Druid rites of ancient Europe. "

Then he pointed towards Orghana's tent and added.

"I suppose that at this moment the fusion of those traditions of the East and the West is being consummated, and that the one in command is that of the East

"This is all unreal." Berglund muttered. Aman replied.

"What happens is that it is part of a different reality than the one you and I know. It is a misty sphere that lies between waking and dreaming, but it is no less real. "

Episode 11

The fire was gradually dying down as the added firewood was consumed. The three men were still together, each deep in thought. Finally Jack affirmed, turning to Aman.

"As you say, in this mission nothing is as it seems, nor is anyone what they told us at the beginning. What can we finally believe?"

Taro thought for a moment and then answered.

"Orghana is indeed a descendant of King Bogd Khan, and we have met her sister Tsegseg. Just as the sister defended with her life the treasure of the ancient king, fighting with her occult arts against her enemies, also Orghana, raised in the same cradle, and with the same powers, will fight to defend the inheritance of Genghis Khan against any other candidate. that appears, whom she will consider an impostor. "

"That is to say that she is not here only as a representative of the CIA, but to fight for the rights of her family." Jack concluded

"That's right. Having personal reasons to fight in this cause ensures that she will appeal to all means to do so, and we still do not know what those means are. " added Aman Bodniev.

"The problem is that since she has an agenda of her own, we cannot be sure that her objectives will always coincide with those of the Bluthund Circle. We must be on guard to detect deviations. " said Jack in a depressed tone. Then he added.

"And what should we think of Ives Richart? Was the story with which he joined our mission also a lie? "

Bodniev replied.

"It was partially true. The man is indeed a scholar in his matter, but he is also an initiate in the Druidic occult arts, and as such he has his hidden agenda as well. Upon finding a priestess of Black Tengrism he immediately submitted to her, and today we must regard him, along with Colonel Khulan, as a subordinate of Orghana. "

Jack analyzed the responses. As head of the expedition he felt the weight of the responsibility to make decisions about the destination of the mission. He finally said.

"It's okay. The truth is that at the moment it seems that the aims of Orghana are compatible with those of the Bluthund Circle, we will continue with our search. I'm going to tell Dr Richardson. "

That said, he got up and went to his tent. Taro did the same, while Bodniev completely extinguished the embers of the fire so that at dawn the column of smoke would not reveal his position to possible enemies.

When he entered his store; Jack Berglund checked his watch, calculated the time difference, and decided to call Richardson in New York City. The Englishman answered immediately.

"William, you're still in your office!" Exclaimed Jack in surprise.

"Yes, today I am behind with my homework. I've ordered some sandwiches and we'll have dinner with Louie at the office. "

Louie was not only the man in charge of the surveillance, but a kind of security adviser to the Bluthund Circle. Jack then shared the news of the day, with special emphasis on the true character of Orghana and Ives Richart.

Richardson pondered for a moment what Berglund had communicated, and then responded.

"Jack. I agree with your evaluation. For now there is no conflict between Orghana's possible motivations and the task entrusted to the Community by Admiral Donnelly. I think you should go ahead with the mission, but don't hesitate to abort it if at any point you find yourselves in danger. "

In another of the tents a soft murmur occurred in the absolute darkness inside. A female voice and a male voice whispered in an ancient primordial language, common to the origins of men in all continents, while a soft noise of hands moving between the sheets could be heard.

"Do you really have magical powers?" The male voice asked.

"You have doubts?"

"Why should I believe? What is the magic? "

"You are here with me, where I want to have you. That is the magic!"

The dawn appeared in the middle of a strong fog. The rays of the sun could not infiltrate the moisture that gushed from the earth, and they produced only a dim and generalized brightness.

Aman Bodniev was the first to wake up, then joined by Khulan and Taro Suzuki. Between them lit a small fire in which they heated breakfast, trusting that the mist would not give away their position to their possible enemies. The rest woke up and joined the collation to get the cold out of their bodies. Finally Jack said.

"We are going out anyway. This fog is very thick and will take time to rise. We will drive very slowly, so that we can see at least a small part of the road. Do you want to let me do the driving? " He asked Ives Richart.

"No, I can do it. I prefer that you act as a navigator pointing the way. "

They put out the fire, raised the dew-damp tents and put them in the truck. They then took their places in the customary seats, Orghana, Jack, and Khulan carrying their automatic weapons at the ready pointed out the vehicle's windows.

The path, which had been slightly uphill up to that point, was beginning to get steeper and the travelers felt the effect of the ascent in their ears. Vision was limited to about ten feet in front of the car, so Ives drove very carefully, around the curves of the trail and the stones in the middle of the road, which obviously no one was taking care of. The Toyota truck's engine needed to push harder for the climb, and Ives had put in the higher-traction gear.

A hole opened high up in the mass of mist, allowing them to see a small patch of clear blue sky. At the same time a breeze began to blow, stirring up the masses of water droplets suspended in the air and forming some local eddies.

"I am hopeful that the haze will lift soon." said cheerfully Ives, who had to strain both his eyes and his foot on the accelerator to drive in those conditions.

"And then we'll see what we find." Taro added skeptically.

At that moment, a strong gust of wind from above shook the immense mass of moisture, carrying it away almost instantly. The contours of the road became effectively visible, as well as the slopes of the surrounding gentle hills.

A scream of terror arose from all six gorges, as they gazed at the now visible hilltops.

A line of mounted Mongol horsemen surrounded them from all three sides, carrying their ancient rifles in their hands.

Episode 12

Seeing the fearsome horsemen facing them with their weapons, located no more than a hundred feet away, terror spread inside the truck. Travelers most seasoned in military action reacted first.

"They are bandits! We must get out of here immediately. " Khulan yelled.

Ives had a moment of uncertainty, suddenly, Jack's voice boomed next to him.

"Run over them! at full speed."

Frenchman immediately snapped out of his stupor and stepped on the gas pedal, putting the powerful Toyota engine at full revs. The tires first skidded on the ground, but then they kicked into gear, blowing smoke from their top layer. The vehicle was thrown over the compact line of riders.

The Mongols directly in front of them, seeing the fireball rush toward them, immediately tried to break away, fleeing in terror in all directions. One of the horses was frightened and failed to obey the command of its rider and as it was in front of the truck was thrown a great distance to the right, while a large bloodstain covered the windshield of the vehicle. Horror spread through the six occupants as they realized the Toyota was speeding past the rider's mangled body.

Ives kept the pressure on the gas pedal to maximum, and the car flew between the cliffs, leaving the line of bandits behind

The Mongols had been disbanded by the unexpected action of the driver, but immediately rebuilt their line, turned their horses towards the opposite direction in which they were and prepared to launch themselves in pursuit of their prey, furious when they saw the end of their companion shattered on the ground.

The truck suddenly reached the top of the cliff and a void appeared in front of it. The inertia of the car's mass was so great that Ives was no longer in control of the vehicle and could only grip the wheel tightly. Again the terror seized the travelers, seeing themselves projected into an abyss that they could not see, because the front of the car was still directed upwards. Vertigo joined fear. Soon the truck lowered its trunk and they could see that they were still in the air but heading into a fairly deep and long green valley, but not a cliff. Everyone held their breath as they realized that in seconds the car would fall to the bottom of the valley, after flying through more than 150 feet, and anticipating that the crash of the fall on the ground could be brutal.

Indeed, when the four wheels hit the ground, a very strong blow was produced on the entire structure of the vehicle that was transmitted to the bodies of its occupants. Fortunately, after the impact, the car continued to roll without breaking into pieces. From inside the truck came a formidable Hooray! of six throats, when verifying that they were still alive.

However, when Taro turned his head back he saw clearly that the bandits had also recovered from their surprise and were running after them at a gallop.

"They are following us and closing in!" The Japanese yelled With desperation.

The fleeing travelers could see the magnificent fighting efficiency of the Mongol horses, whose hooves barely touched the ground at the speed of their movement. A bullet from behind pierced the rear window of the truck. Indeed, one of the fighting characteristics of Mongolian horsemen has always been the experience of firing their rifles at full gallop on the backs of their horses.

One of the bandits had taken advantage of the others and was approaching from the right of the vehicle. From the passenger seat, Jack saw the Mongol clearly, so close that he could make out his features. The bandit readied his rifle and Jack Berglund readied his. Both fired at the same time, and once the effect of the flash on the truck had passed, the occupants could see the rider collapsing from his animal, which, still thrown at full speed, dragged him hanging from a stirrup for a long time.

Bodniev patted Jack's shoulder, saying.

"I see that you retain your aim despite the time elapsed."

"Mongol training is never forgotten, but neither is that of the Marines." Answered the American.

But the situation was not improving for the fugitives. The Toyota was already running through the lower part of the valley, which luckily did not offer obstacles to its movement, but it was already approaching the next peak, behind which no one knew what was hiding.

"We were saved because although perhaps the bandits were ambushed waiting for us, they too were completely covered by the mist and did not see us coming. They could not hear the engine noise either, because we were coming at low speed and the fog absorbs the sounds. When the haze suddenly lifted, they were as surprised by our appearance as we were. "

Such was the explanation given by Bodniev to his comrades of what happened minutes before. Behind them the pursuers continued firing, but most of their bullets missed their target, although some hit the car body, but without causing injury or damage to the vehicle.

The slope was now decidedly upward, and again the engine had to struggle to overcome the law of gravity, but for the moment it was maintaining speed.

"For the bandits, too, the slope is upward, and there is no doubt that their horses must already be feeling the exhaustion of this pursuit." Said Taro. Bodniev, who was sitting behind the driver, this time patted Ives on the shoulder saying.

"I have to admit that you have shown nerves of steel. Few drivers would have come out of this horrible situation. "

Instead of answering the compliment, the Frenchman pointed his head forward, saying.

"We are already nearing the top and what I see is a stone wall in front of us. I do not know where we will pass. This is where our escape may end. "

However Jack pointed a little to the left, expressing.

"There is a narrow gorge at ground level between the rocks. It is a kind of natural window. Head there. "

The driver slightly deviated his course and they found that indeed a cleft was opening in the solid rock.

"I hope it's wide enough to let the car pass." Said Ives, as Orghana muttered a prayer in the lost language she used in her religious practices. Khulan, who was looking back at the pursuers, suddenly screamed.

"Something happens! The bandits are stopping their horses and gesturing ahead of us. They are abandoning the chase. "

The Colonel's phrase produced momentary relief, but almost immediately Orghana screamed.

"Oh no! Not again."

Episode 13

Desperate, Ives looked at Jack for waiting for instructions, but the American shook his head and said.

"No, this time we can't resist; we wouldn't have a chance. "

Taro from the back seat added.

"Furthermore, we do not know their intentions. They certainly didn't know we were coming here, so an ambush like that of the bandits is out of the question. "

"I'm going to go out of the car and talk to them and find out who they are." Said Khulan, opening the rear door of the vehicle and getting out with his hands up, after putting the rifle on the seat. He approached what instinctively seemed to be the leader of the group, an imposing Mongol, with two cartridge belts crossed over his chest and a fearsome Kalashnikov in his hands. The remaining travelers saw the Colonel negotiate with the man and soon return to the car. He opened the door and said.

"They are sentinels on guard to prevent bandits or any other intruder from entering the lands where they have been installed for two years. They belong to a tribe of Khalkha ethnic origin, which have been ruled by the Borjigin Khans, a noble sub-clan that provided princes and princesses to Mongolia until the beginning of the 20th century. "

"Tribes, clans, Khalkha ... what all this means to us." Asked Jack confused.

"It is part of the ethnic mosaic of Mongolia." Khulan replied. "But what is truly important is that Orghana and her family are part of the Borjigin clan, of which these tribes have been vassals for centuries."

"Is that good news?" asked Ives.

"They can be. I explained who Princess Orghana is to the man I spoke to. This man is just one of the sergeants of the chieftain of the tribe. He has already sent an emissary on horseback to ask for instructions. The chieftain is called Temük Khan, and is quite powerful because he commands a large group of tribes scattered in this area. The central camp is in the next valley, which is quite wide. For that reason they have a strict control of who approaches from the east. For now we are going to camp here and have lunch to wait for instructions. "

"Good idea. Perhaps we can invite this sergeant to win his goodwill. " expressed Aman Bodniev.

"I'm going to invite him." Khulan replied. After a while he came back and said.

"The sergeant does not accept because he does not want his men to see him eating, and because of his number, not everyone can participate in the lunch. It would create resentments. "

"Fine, but there's one thing he's not going to refuse." Aman said as he sneakily extracted a small bottle of vodka from his clothes.

"Tell him to come over to the truck."

They were eating trying to hide behind the truck so as not to offend the sentries. The scene was one of slight tension for not knowing how the trip was going to end, but in general the attitude of the tribesmen was not hostile.

After two hours the sergeant came up and said. "Temük Khan wants to meet Princess Orghana. He has met her mother, the High Priestess, in the past. You will all be able to go but I must withdraw your weapons, which will be returned to you when they leave our camp. "...

The travelers disassembled the precarious camp they had made to eat, put out the fire, reluctantly handed their weapons to the sergeant, who told them.

"Now get in the vehicle and follow my emissary to the central camp. Drive very slowly at all times. "

Aman Bodniev slipped the vodka bottle into the sergeant's pocket, who pretended not to notice.

As soon as they crossed the top of the hill with the vehicle, the picture changed completely. A wide flat valley opened between the mountain ranges that rose on both sides, forming a large grazing field, in which scattered groups of Mongolian cows were seen, cared for by few muleteers, some of them children, and by flocks of dogs.

In general, the landscape struck travelers as smiling, particularly after so many worries in the previous hours. Orghana's eyes blazed with excitement as she found herself back in the deep heart of her native Mongolia, and Colonel Khulan looked at her with pleasure. As they advanced towards the center of the valley, the dwellings, at first very far from each other, became more numerous and larger, possibly due to the presence of more important families.

The travelers carefully observed the yurts, the traditional transportable dwellings of the Mongols and other Central Asian peoples, made up of a framework of wood that was arranged on a circular plan, forming a cylinder of large diameter and not too high above the ground, with increasing height towards the center. This structure is then covered with woolen canvases and fabrics, and sometimes with straw, allowing the inhabitants to add or remove layers according to the season of the year and thus withstand the harsh Mongolian winters. This type of housing, easily dismantled and carried, constitutes an essential element of the nomadic lifestyle of some of the Mongolian tribes still today. Women were in the past responsible for assembling and disassembling yurts, and working three or four women could assemble a yurt in a couple of hours. However, since the long migrations of the tribes become increasingly spaced, some of the yurts built today do not have the ephemeral character of the past, and although they retain the general shape, they are made of other more evolved materials, and they have details of greater comfort for its dwellers, including internal divisions to give privacy to family members.

Mongols of both sexes and all ages circulated among the yurts, dressed in the showy tunics that they wear over their pants and other undergarments. These tunics are adapted to cold climates, and are dyed in bright colors, often with beautiful embroidery of warm-colored threads. The men cover their heads with the classic cylindrical fur caps and the young women usually have on their heads headdresses made with beads and other elements. In general, Mongolian clothing, particularly of the more prosperous, has a high degree of home craftsmanship.

Men of all ages walked leading the small and agile Mongolian horses, with their mounts also with handcrafted details. Many camels sat in the sun, waiting to be loaded to start the long marches of the merchants who carried out commercial exchanges between the tribes linked to each other.

The horseman who guided the travelers was greeted by the men he encountered, demonstrating the close bond between the members of the tribe. Finally they arrived in front of a large white yurt, around which some women were doing kitchen work or embroidering, sitting in the sun, while children of various ages were engaged in their games, which from what the travelers could discern, were scenes of war . The guide dismounted from his horse and told them.

"You can get out of the vehicle. In moments you will be greeted by Temük Khan. "

A tense expectation opened for the travelers, whose fate depended critically on the attitude of the powerful Mongol chief.

Episode 14

AFTER A CAREFULLY STUDIED delay, Chief Temük appeared at the door of his yurt, accompanied by who was undoubtedly his wife. Both moved with the elegance that one would expect in a 19th century

European royal court. The two spouses were dressed in identical garments, although logically adapted to the size and sex of each one. A fine tunic carefully embroidered with gold, blue and black threads covered all the clothing they wore underneath. The sleeves, neck, and lower edges of the tunic were blue, the same color as the embroidery. The Khan wore a blue sash at the waist, and had a cap made of the same fabric as the tunic with a blue velvet lining. His boots were lined on the outside with black fabric exquisitely embroidered with scrolls of gold thread.

From the hat of the same design of the wife hung a kind of braids of shiny beads, also repeating the color design of the whole outfit. The lady's waist was slim, and she had a gentle smile on her beautiful face. The Khan's appearance was haughty but not shocking. A more dazzling royal couple could hardly be found anywhere on Earth.

Following an implicit protocol, everyone remained silent until the Khan decided to break it. Addressing Orghana he said in Mongolian.

"You must be the daughter of the High Priestess of our cult that I knew in my youth. You have the same air and the same features. "

Reassured by the implicit realization that Temük Khan was a follower of Black Tengrism, thus creating a bond between the two, Orghana replied in a respectful but not subservient voice.

"That's right, Khan. I remember my mother talking about you in my childhood. " Of course that statement was not true.

Temük went on to say in his neutral tone.

"I remember the Priestess coming with a beautiful little girl. Was it you? "

"I don't remember coming to their lands. She must have been my older sister Tsegseg. "

"Ah! Yes, I remember that name. How is she?"

"Well, when my mother retired, Tsegseg was appointed as her successor by the Council of Elders of Tengrism. She is totally dedicated to worship and caring for her family. "

"Do they live in Ulan Bator?"

"No. When there were many riots in Mongolia Tsegseg moved to France. She comes to this country twice a year. "

Khulan translated into English for travelers, and Ives paid particular attention to the ignored details of the life of his beloved.

With a very gentle gesture the Khan said.

"This lady is my beloved wife, *Begum* Altansarnai, whose name means Golden Rose."

All travelers bow their heads respectfully to the lady, who without stopping smiling said to her husband.

"My dear Temük, are you going to continue talking to our visitors at the door of the house, or are you going to show them to our abode?"

Not at all bothered by the gentle rebuke of his wife, Temük Khan indicated with his arm the inside of the wide yurt saying.

"Of course. You will see how fortunate I am to have a wife who helps me with the tasks of conducting the affairs of my tribe. Please come to my humble home. "

Only when entering the *ger* or *yurt*, travelers realized the spaciousness and interior comfort of the house. Its circular shape provides a spatial sensation very different from that of western rooms, which are in general square or rectangular. Most of the timbers that make up the walls of the yurt were covered by furniture, some of traditional Mongolian inspiration and others of functional western design. The visitors were struck by the fact that the floor of the house was covered with decorated ceramic tiles, which is not to be expected in a supposedly transitory house of nomadic tribes. On the tiles, wide rugs covered parts of them, where there were large armchairs and even parts of the walls covered by rugs.

The yurt they entered was certainly not the only one belonging to the Khan and Begum marriage, as it was actually a large living room, with the dining room on one side, fitted with a large rectangular table. The center was occupied by a stove or heater of the type called salamander, from which emerged a long vertical metal pipe that reached the apex of the conical roof, acting as a breather for the house, and as an outlet for heating and cooking fumes.

On the side opposite the door was a cupboard in which crockery and tablecloths were kept.

Begum Altansarnai herself went to a kettle in which she was heating water on the stove and poured into the cups that were waiting on the table.

Colonel Khulan spoke first in Mongolian and then in English.

"Temük Khan invites us to share his tea, the highest symbol of Mongolian hospitality. Please, sit down."

The tea ceremony was formal, following strict oriental protocol, and the *Begum* was in charge of directing it in her capacity of housewife. For half an hour Temük Khan and his guests exchanged memories of the past.

At one point, the hostess lifted the dishes and left the yurt pretending other activities, but with the obvious purpose of letting her husband find out the reason for the presence of the distinguished guests in the camp. Indeed, the Khan was guiding the conversation with great skill towards the trip of his guests to that location, lost in the mountains of Mongolia.

Khulan glanced at Orghana, who gave him a slight nod, in accordance with some implicit gestural code between them.

The Colonel came directly into the topic.

"Honorable Temük Khan. Undoubtedly you must wonder why a direct descendant of our illustrious King Bogd Khan has appeared in your camp, especially without an adequate escort, and in the way in which our arrival to their lands occurred, pursued by a group of bandits who came close to killing us all. "

"As you can imagine, only powerful and urgent reasons could have compelled us to make this journey."

They all realized that Khulan had captured the host's full attention. The Colonel continued.

"I am going to ask Princess Orghana to explain these reasons herself."

Episode 15

The visitors were excited to learn that Orghana was going to explain to the powerful tribal chief the reasons for their presence in the isolated mountains of central Mongolia.

They already knew that the young woman was a source of surprises so they wanted to hear what new revelations she would make.

The lady fixed her eyes on Temük Khan's. She got straight to the point.

"Members of my family have heard rumors that a certain chief who calls himself Baatar, and therefore pretends to be a Hero directly descended from Genghis Khan, is stirring up the scattered nomadic tribes, and inciting them to an armed pan-Mongol general uprising against established nations in the region, such as the Republic of Mongolia, China, the Russian Federation and Kazakhstan. This impostor and the true instigators behind him argue that if they can unify all the tribes they can generate a wave like the one that centuries ago led Genghis Khan and his successors to create the largest Empire of all time. This wild proclamation can only lead to a bloodbath throughout Central and East Asia, like the one Genghis Khan himself provoked in his time, in what was one of the greatest carnage of all time. Only today, such a movement would rally against it all the great powers of the world, including not only China and Russia, but also the United States and Europe. The uprising would be destroyed with the enormous military means of those powers, and a good part of the Mongolian people would be mercilessly annihilated."

Orghana was obviously excited; before continuing, she took a drink from the glass of water that the Begum had left for each attendee, and then she continued.

"In our capacity of legitimate descendants of King Bogd Khan, and therefore of Genghis Khan, the members of my family headed by my mother and my sister Tsegseg, that is, the former and the current Supreme Priestesses of our religion, have taken over the mission to abort this tragic uprising. Because of my age and my training, I was the one designated to carry out this purpose. Since the interests of the CIA of the United States go in the same direction, I have been included by them in the mission of the Bluthund Circle. Together with my colleagues here present, our task is to obtain information that will make it possible to thwart this uprising."

The density of the young woman's explanation was very great, as well as the implications of her revelation. All the assistants had been left breathless and therefore they took some time to reflect on what was exposed by the Princess. Jack was unaware that the CIA, and perhaps the Bluthund Circle authorities, were aware of the young woman's true personality, and wondered somewhat annoyed if Richardson knew, and in that case why he had not told him, despite Berglund being the boss of the mission. Ives was once again in awe of the true personality of the woman he loved, as well as her eloquence. Taro Suzuki and Aman Bodniev pondered the roles of each of those present, and the true scope of what seemed like a routine spy mission in Asia.

Temük Khan was silent, no doubt because his head was processing everything he heard, and the others respected that silence. Finally the tribal chief spoke.

"Of course, the members of the council of elders of my tribe are aware of the movements of the henchmen of the so-called Baatar, and we have great concern and fear for the breakdown of the peace between us, which is always fragile."

At that moment the Begum reentered yurt. Without saying a word or asking her husband's permission, she sat down at the table and prepared to participate in the meeting. Taro Suzuki, a fine observer of attitudes and protocols, confirmed his assumption that the lady was not a passive and modest person, according to the role she played, but an important member in the direction of the affairs of the tribe, which her husband had already advanced. Seeing his wife present at the meeting, Temük Khan's voice changed and sounded more confident. He continued saying.

"In this valley we are surrounded by warlike and unstable tribes, among which Baatar has been preaching. We cannot place ourselves in a frankly antagonistic position with theirs because we want to preserve that peace of which I spoke. However, you can count on the protection of me and my tribe when you are in my territories. It's the least we can do out of respect for your mother and your family. "

The Begum lips showed a pleased smile. The travelers welcomed the news, as although the Khan made no commitment to actively support them in their mission, he at least provided them with a safe haven during their stay.

The talk went on and it was getting dark outside. Temük Khan finally told the visitors around him.

"Tomorrow we have organized an exhibition of Mongolian horsemen for your benefit. I hope you will honor us with your presence. "

Taro Suzuki, obviously excited by the proposal, rushed to reply on behalf of everyone.

"Yes, of course, we will be delighted to see the feats of the famous Mongol horsemen."

Aman Bodniev added.

"Mr. Suzuki is a reknown Japanese martial arts teacher. He maybe can enrich the parade, for example, by exhibiting a kata. "

"Ah! Wonderful idea." replied the Begum.

The visitors were able to stay in three yurts that had interior subdivisions, prepared for people who were temporarily in the camp.

Left alone in his room, Jack Berglund picked up his satellite phone and contacted Dr. Richardson in New York. He then recounted everything that had happened, including the revelations made by Orghana about the commission given by the CIA in her capacity as belonging to an important Mongolian family. The English listened to him with concern.

"Sorry Jack, I had no idea that Lady Orghana already had an agreed mission with the CIA. Otherwise I would have told you, since in your capacity as head of the mission it is up to you to know. This Donnelly old fox never told me."

Episode 16

When at midmorning the next day they were summoned by Temük Khan's emissary and taken to a great plain stretching two hundred paces from the center of the camp, they were unprepared for the spectacle that unfolded before their eyes.

Located side by side in a perfect line, a hundred Mongol horsemen stood expectantly awaiting orders from their chief, who was sitting with his wife and other members of his family in a kind of box set up on the side of the plain.

Temük Khan and the Begum wore formal clothes that gave an account of their superior status, but had an unquestionable military connotation. The box was covered by a red canopy with multicolored decorations and pieces of cloth with texts written in the Mongolian alphabet with meanings that the visitors did not understand.

The riders, who remained motionless, were mounted on their horses with luxurious saddles, each one carried in his right hand a long spear with a standard at the end, while in his left hanhe had the reins of his horse and a small circular metal shield with various geometric designs.

The breeze made the banners and the messages written on the cloth bands sway. The riders as well as the approximately two hundred standing spectators remained silent, giving the entire scene a solemn character.

At one point, Temük Khan, located about a hundred paces from the place assigned to the visitors, stood up and raised a ceremonial saber over his head, in a gesture that started the show.

THE LINE OF HORSEMEN began to move slowly, spreading across
the plain, until they were aligned again but transversely to what they
had been before. Then, an official who was next to the chieftain's box
blew a metal horn, and all the vertigo was triggered instantly. A cry
arose from a hundred throats and a hundred horses, estimulated by
the spurs of their riders, galloped off towards the center of the plain.
The horsemen carried their spears pointed forward in a classic cavalry
charge position on an imaginary enemy located in front of them.
Indeed, wooden poles covered in ox skins loomed about two hundred

yards ahead in the path of the attacking horde. As they passed the posts, the horsemen drove their spears into them, and when the dust raised by the horses' hooves settled, the travelers could see the pieces of wood bristling with spears with their banners dangling. A chill ran down the spine of the outsiders at the fearsome charge of the Mongol horsemen. Jack Berglund and his companions understood the terror inspired seven centuries earlier by the Mongols' predecessors in populations throughout Asia and at the gates of Europe.

The riders, upon reaching an imaginary line located about five hundred yards ahead, suddenly stopped their gallop and turned their direction 180 degrees, facing the point from which they had started. After a new sound of the horn, the riders drew their sabers from their pods and galloped in reverse, swinging their weapons overhead as they shouted their war slogans. The savage spectacle reached its climax when the warriors again passed in front of the posts and, raising their sabers, they unloaded them on the posts, severing the shafts of the spears, so that after the passage of the new cavalry charge, none of the spears were nailed to the posts.

A formidable Hurray rose from the throats of the spectators, as they saw the fearsome efficiency of their riders. Temük Khan rose from his chair and took a few steps, saluting the formidable group of warriors of his tribe with his staff.

Taro Suzuki couldn't control his enthusiasm and stood up to join the ovation, despite his usually controlled temperament and aloof from emotional reactions; he was followed by Jack Berglund, Ives Richart and Aman Bodniev. After the first moment of admiration, it was the Frenchman who noticed the absences.

"Where is Orghana? And where is Khulan? "

The remaining travelers looked at each other in surprise; none had paid attention to anything other than the contingent of horsemen and their exploits.

Suddenly, Jack said, pointing once more to the plain.

"Look there. Who is that?"

As the others looked in the direction indicated by the American, they saw an isolated horseman galloping across the now empty plain, before the surprised gaze of the authorities in the box, the one hundred Mongol horsemen and the two hundred spectators, who gave the show for finished.

It was Ives who recognized, against all expectations, the rider.

"I can't believe it! It's Orghana!"

Straining their eyes, the remaining visitors could indeed recognize in the small mounted figure the companion of recent adventures.

The Princess spurred her mount into a tent where, planted on the ground with their points down, were a series of spears like the ones the horsemen had carried in their charge against the wooden posts.

With a jerk, Orghana raised one of the javelins and, with it in hand, sped toward the wooden targets. The horse's legs were barely visible from the speed of the gallop, and soon the figure was engulfed in the cloud of dust raised by the hooves. The woman went towards one of the posts that was in the middle of the transversal row, and without moving her body to the sides drove the spear into half the diameter of the trunk.

A clamor rose from the three hundred gorges that lined the equestrian maneuvering track. Tears welled up in Ives Richart's eyes as his companions hoarse from exclamations.

As had happened before with the hundred horsemen, Orghana and his steed surpassed the place where the posts were. The woman restrained the horse, made it change front and gallop again towards the posts, but this time from the opposite end. As she approached the target where she had driven her javelin, the woman drew a saber from the scabbard that hung from the mount and swung it over her head. She sped past the side of the post, and once she had gotten past that position back, everyone could see that the spear planted in the wood was gone and only a stump remained in the wood.

Faced with this show of skill, the reaction of the attendees bordered on delirium, the Mongolian fur hats flew through the air and the children danced among themselves.

Ecstatic, Temük Khan wiped his eyes with the edge of his hand. With his fine intuition he understood that he had witnessed the birth of a new myth of his people, this time at the hands of one of the famous Mongolian femalewarriors, whose feats sang the traditions that came from the bottom of history, long before Genghis Khan.

Episode 17

At the end of her tour around the posts, Orghana put the saber in its scabbard but did not return to where her companions were; she directed instead her horse to a place close to that of Temük Khan's box.

Jack, Taro, Ives and Aman followed her activities with their eyes, and soon they saw that when the woman stopped the horse, Colonel Khulan approached her and handed her something that they could not see from the distance.

Upon receiving it, the Princess again prodded the steed, which galloped off again in the direction of the posts. The companions could see that as she approached the static targets, the rider was leaning over the left side of the horse's neck and when she was still about sixty yards away from the center post she was holding with an arm an bow; the other arm stretched out the rope on which a long feathered arrow had already been attached. The horse raced about twenty yards at full speed while the woman only held onto her saddle with her knees.

The arrow was launched with great force due to the tension of the bow, and hit the middle of the post, where it stayed oscillating due to the energy that had been communicated to it by the archer's arm.

Seeing the feat, the crowd broke into shouting, in a new hurray, maddened to see that the young stranger had mastered the ultimate technique that distinguished Mongol horsemen in the time of Genghis Khan, when hitting a small target with an arrow thrown with bow from a galloping horse.

IVES JUMPED WITH EXCITEMENT and went to hug an octogenarian Mongolian who had just thrown his fur hat into the air. Although the Frenchman could not understand him, the old man told him that as a child he had heard of this feat, but had never seen it carried out.

When Temük Khan had controlled his enthusiasm and returned to his seat in the box next to his wife, he looked the Begum in the eye and asked her.

"Is this her?"

The lady smiled sweetly at her husband and replied.

"Yes, dear husband. This is the pristess that you have been waiting for all your life, and now she has appeared in your lands and in our lives."

When Orghana finished her show of mounted archery, she made with her horse a wide circle around the plain where the spectators had gathered to watch the show. They all gave her an excited applause when they saw materialize the traditions that the elders had told them. Finally she arrived on her circular route in front of Temük Khan's box and at that moment the animal decided to raise its front legs, leaning only on the back ones.

The Princess greeted the authorities in the box by raising the bow on her outstretched right arm. Then she calmed the excited horse and dismounted, taking a few steps toward the Khan and his wife, then dropped to one knee.

Immediately Temük got up from his seat and ran to his guest, took her by the hand and made her stand up, while the Begum also approached the young woman and took her by the other hand. The couple accompanied Orghana to the box, where another seat had already been placed next to those of Temük and his wife. At that moment both the Khan and his wife raised both Orghana´s arms, greeting the attendees. A long standing ovation approved the symbolic act.

Jack, Ives, Taro and Aman watched the scene from afar, and although they could not fully understand what was happening, at least they interpreted that their partner was being admitted into the inner circle of the powerful Mongol chieftain.

"Orghana has seduced Temük Khan, his wife and his court. This creates a new bond with them. " Ives said hopefully.

"But it can also create new limitations on our mission." replied Taro in a somewhat skeptical tone.

"What do you mean?" Asked Jack.

"Chief Temük will not allow our activities to endanger the stability and peace of his people."

"That's true." Aman admitted. "Especially because we came to investigate a topic with great symbolism for the Mongols."

Once the excitement produced by the military exhibition and the unexpected turn produced by

Orghana's performance, the spectators began to return to their homes, the courtiers dismantled the box, and the travelers also returned to the yurt that had been assigned to them. A cold wind was beginning to blow from the north, erasing the tracks of horses and men on the plain.

Jack and Aman began to improvise a dinner with several different types of food that they brought in their luggage.

Ives was nervous at not hearing from the Princess and Taro tried to reassure him.

"Your lady cannot be in better company." He said.

Aman, who was witnessing the scene in silence, whispered in Jack's ear.

"I hope that doesn't change the girl's attitude towards us and our mission."

Aman had fanned the fire in the furnace in the center of the yurt when an emissary appeared at the door of the house. Jack invited him in; it was an officer of the Khan's troops in ceremonial uniform. The man said directly.

"The Khan invites you to dine in his yurt, then participate in a meeting with the Council of Elders of our tribe."

Faced with Jack's hesitant attitude, Taro hastened to reply in a formal tone.

"Please tell the Khan that we gladly accept the gracious invitation, and the honor that it represents."

When the officer had left, Aman explained the answer given by the martial arts teacher.

"There is a difference between this invitation and the lunch we share with the Khan and the Begum at noon. This was a courtesy based on traditional Mongolian hospitality, with no other meaning or commitment. This current invitation is the entry into a meeting of the group that decides the destinies of this important tribe. The Khan and his wife have decided to put Orghana under their pretense wing, but they have yet to convince the elders, who are precisely those who have chosen him as the great Khan. "

Episode 18

At dinner time, the officer who had conveyed Temük Khan's invitation returned. He was now dressed in full dress uniform, so Bodniev assumed that he was a high-ranking military man in the Khan's small army. They accompanied him walking about three hundred steps to the yurt that Temük used in his receptions and that the survivors already knew. As they approached, the exquisite aroma of meat being cooked on the spit reached their nostrils, and indeed they saw at a short distance from the house some men roasting various pieces of meat on iron rods in the shape of a cross driven into the ground.

When they entered the main yurt, the attendees were already organized around a long rectangular table. At one end of it sat Temük Khan and the Begum, and on either side of them were several younger people, no doubt relatives of the couple; other dignitaries sat on both long sides of the table, and at the opposite end were Orghana and the Colonel Khulan.

Taro, always attentive to orientation protocols, whispered to Jack.

"The most important places are at both ends of the table. Here in one of them sit the Khan and his wife, and in the other Orghana. It is a very clear message of the importance of our partner. "

Not only did her location at the table denote the status of the young woman; the garment she wore was fit for an oriental princess, and by similarity to that worn by the Begum, it left no doubt that Orghana's garment was a loan from the Khan's wife.

The conversation was pointless at first, while the dinner plates were being served, but when it was time for the tea service, quite a ceremony,

Temük Khan began to speak in a higher tone, so that the rest of the diners, about thirty people, fell silent.

"Today we have been fortunate and we could see how Princess Orghana, here by my side today, has put us in touch with our traditions of warrior amazons, and has given us back a joy that we had not experienced for a long time. But Orghana has not come to our camp only to remind us of our origins in the time of the Great Genghis Khan.

"Mainly she has come to unmask the impostors who are stirring up the tribes with false proclamations and lying promises, which can only bring about the ruin of our people, the end of the prosperous times we currently enjoy, and the outpouring of rivers of blood."

Temük looked in the direction of the section of the table where the elders of the Governing Council were sitting. Since he had known them well for many years, he knew immediately that his words expressed the same thoughts as all of them had in their heads. All feared the course of events that the arrival of the agitator known as Baatar would unleash, because they knew that challenging the highest powers in Asia would only lead to a dire end for the Mongolian people.

But on the other hand they also knew that they did not have the means to effectively oppose that messianic leadership, which knew how to gain the fanatical adherence of tribal chiefs lacking in intelligence and prudence.

Basically, what the elders lacked and ultimately Temük was also lacking was an alternative leader who could oppose Baatar in front of the masses of Mongol tribesmen. Because of this, the wiser elders had grasped what had changed so quickly with the sudden appearance of the young Orghana among them, especially knowing that she belonged to the lineage of King Bogd Khan.

As usual, Taro Suzuki, a skilled interpreter of situations relating to Eastern traditions that he was a part of, captured the essence of his host Temük Khan's purpose by organizing this dinner together with

Orghana and prominent members of his tribe. He approached Jack Berglund who was sitting next to him, and whispered to him.

"Our companion, Princess Orghana, is precisely the cement that these tribes need to stand against the dangers that threaten them."

At the end of Temük Khan's speech, the eyes of all the attendees turned to the newly known Princess, obviously with the expectation that she would address them a message. Orghana rose from her chair, and only then did her companions see the transformation that had occurred in her appearance and attitude. The finely embroidered tunic with blue and gold threads fitted her waist and made her appear taller. Her face showed immense inner peace and her eyes showed an intense brilliance. Despite the fact that she had to lecture before an audience that was unknown and who undoubtedly expected a lot from her, the young woman did not seem to have any anxiety. In reality, this was the event of her public manifestation before her people for which she had prepared all her life. Orghana sensed that from that moment on, she ceased to be a CIA agent, an adventurer related to the Bluthund Circle, or any other role that she had had up to that moment, and became, by legitimate dynastic right, the leader of the renewal of all Mongols, a role rarely played by men, and never by a woman before.

Colonel Khulan had approached the travelers and had translated the gist of Temük Khan's lecture. Again, it was Taro Suzuki who fully interpreted the historical chapter Orghana continued her speech by recalling anecdotes from the Mongol people's warrior past, taught to her and her sister by her Mother, the former High Priestess. She narrated them in the same details that she had learned and memorized as a child, which delighted the elders of the Tribe Council, who had not heard these tales for a long time, when the last priests of Black Tengrism had had to flee through the streets. persecutions of the Chinese. Finally, when she was already convinced that she had obtained the attention of the elders, the woman she began to show her cards. "... But we must be sure that the tribesmen will recognize us as the true heirs of

Genghis Khan, and turn their backs on Baatar. For this there is only one way to find an irrefutable argument that proves our identity ... " The girl, with great theatrical sense, did a few moments of silence to suspend her speech. She then she continued speaking. "We need to find the true location of Genghis Khan's tomb, and we need to prove beyond doubt that the one buried there is the Great Chief." A whisper escaped thirty throats upon hearing the lady's bold gamble. This was followed by a few moments of deliberation among the Council elders. Finally, the oldest of them all, undoubtedly the primus inter pares, rose from his chair and said. "It is the opinion of this Council that Princess Orghana's proposal is acceptable, on the condition that the search is carried out discreetly so as not to warn Baatar and his henchmen ahead of time, giving them the possibility not only to abort mission, but also to retaliate against our people in this valley, before we are ready to defend ourselves. " Then, this time addressing Temük Khan, he added. "The Council authorizes you to carry out the proposed mission to find the tomb of the Genghis Khan, on the condition I mentioned."companions, who observed his attitudes, imitated him and concentrated on the effect that the words the woman would pronounce would have on the present, since they depended on Khulan's translation to understand the message.

Orghana began to speak, her voice sounded firm and vibrant, even if she was excited it was obvious that she was in total control of her feelings.

"Fate, with its infinite wisdom, which surpasses the plans that humans can draw in our ignorance, has wanted to bring me to this place, and put me in the care of your leader Temük Khan and his Council of Elders, who direct with great skill this important tribe in difficult times, in the midst of the turbulence produced by our past and the present of our Nation ... "

Episode 19

O rghana continued her speech by recalling anecdotes from the Mongol people's warrior past, taught to her and her sister by her Mother, the former High Priestess. She narrated them in the same details that she had learned and memorized as a child, which delighted the elders of the Tribe Council, who had not heard these tales for a long time, when the last priests of Black Tengrism had had to flee due to the religious persecutions of the Chinese.

Finally, when she was already convinced that she had obtained the attention of the elders, the woman began to show her cards.

"... But we must be sure that the tribesmen will recognize us as the true heirs of Genghis Khan, and turn their backs on Baatar. To achieve this there is only one way, to find an irrefutable argument that proves our identity ... "

The girl, with great theatrical sense, did a few moments of silence and suspended her speech, then she continued speaking.

"We need to find the true location of Genghis Khan's tomb, and we need to prove beyond doubt that the one buried there is the Great Chief."

A whisper escaped thirty throats upon hearing the lady's bold move. This was followed by a few moments of deliberation among the Council elders. Finally, the oldest of them all, undoubtedly the *primus inter pares*, rose from his chair and said.

"It is the opinion of this Council that Princess Orghana's proposal is acceptable, on the condition that the search is carried out discreetly so as not to warn Baatar and his henchmen ahead of time, giving them the possibility not only to abort the mission, but also to retaliate against our people in this valley, before we are ready to defend ourselves. "

Then, this time addressing Temük Khan, he added.

"The Council authorizes you to carry out the proposed mission to find the tomb of the Genghis Khan, on the condition I mentioned."

The old man sat down and this time it was Temük who stood up.

"I find the Council's recommendation very wise and prudent, and I entrust Princess Orghana with the mission of searching and finding the Great Chief's tomb, with an additional condition that I add at this time. When it is actually found, the control and surveillance of the site will be in charge of our tribe. I will select twenty warriors from among the bravest and most experienced of our men to provide protection for Lady Orghana and her companions. They will be at the command of my nephew Altan, whom everyone knows."

A new murmur of approval ran through the yurt. Again Taro Suzuki whispered in his friend Jack Berglund's ear.

"I think that the appointed chief's nephew Altan will have another mission besides protecting our team."

"What do you mean?"

"I think that Altan must ensure that the benefits of the discovery of Genghis Khan's tomb go to Temük Khan and his tribe, and not to others."

The American smiled and replied.

"Good reflection, Taro. I appreciate your lucidity. I don't know what I would do without you. "

The meeting lasted a little longer and then everyone present went to their homes. As he walked to the yurt he shared with Suzuki, Jack was talking to the recorder in his hand in order to. As he walked to the yurt he shared with Suzuki, Jack was talking to his recorder in order to draft a report for William Richardson, the president of the Bluthund Circle. Hearing himself reviewing what had happened that night, realized that the Englishman was going to ask many questions that he could not answer.

Hearing his yurtmate's argument with the boss in New York, Taro decided to go for a walk to give his friend more privacy. As he left the dwelling he saw a shadow heading towards the house that had been assigned to Princess Orghana. Then it waited a moment at the door, until it opened and Taro could fleetingly see the woman inside, still dressed in her ceremonial robe; then the shadow entered the yurt and the door closed behind it; Taro had no doubt that the man he had seen from behind was Ives Richard, unmistakable for his tall stature and slim figure. A smile appeared on the Japanese man's lips. Behind the hardened martial arts master was a romantic spirit.

Just as the American had anticipated, Dr. Richardson was giving him a hard time with his questions.

"So not only did Orghana have her own agenda in Mongolia, but she also had a perfectly established plan to achieve her goals. It is actually she who has been using the CIA and our Bluthund Circle to carry out her plans, and not the other way around. "

"I don't think there was a detailed plan foreseen in advance." Jack replied. "Don't forget that we came to the valley occupied by Temük Khan and his tribe, pursued by Mongol bandits, and that it was upon entering their domain that we found refuge. There is a strong element of randomness in everything that happened. The bandits could have caught up with us and our bones would be in the dust of the steppe if the sentinels of Temük did not appear. "

The Englishman yielded to the evidence, yet insisted.

"I have to speak to Admiral Donnelly. It is one thing to search for the grave of a leader who died eight hundred years ago, and another thing to put ourselves at the head of a counter-movement that could drag the entire area into a civil war. "

"Where are the interests of the Western world?" Inquired Jack.

"That is what I do not know. Furthermore, all this occurs on the very borders of the Russian Federation and the People's Republic of China. You know how they get paranoid every time someone intrudes on their backyard. "

"Something like the reissue of the Great Game between the English and Russian Empires in the 19th century."

"Yes, although in another region of Asia, not in India in the time of Rudyard Kipling."

Exhausted, Jack leaned out of a yurt window. From there he could see Orghana's dwelling, and between the curtains he could see the shadows of two bodies with a weak light coming from behind. Also he, guessed the Frenchman's silhouette. Matsuko's small figure came to his memory and he sighed for not being able to spend with her the same moments that the Princess and Ives were enjoying her. At that moment he heard that Taro was returning to the yurt they shared; Jack closed the window and got into bed.

Episode 20

It took Temük Khan two days to prepare the group of warriors that would accompany the travelers in their search for the tomb of Genghis Khan. All the young men of the tribe were vying for the honor of being part of the event, since in recent times Temük's subjects had rarely left their territory and they all had an insatiable thirst for adventure. Also, serving alongside a young heroine who had dazzled them with her prowess was inspiring.

The caravan set in motion in the early hours of a Thursday morning, after a very cold night that demanded a strong and hot breakfast.

In front of the truck carrying some of the travelers and all their provisions marched four warriors under the command of Colonel Khulan, whose rank had been recognized by Temük and the Council elders. Behind the vanguard Orghana rode likewise escorted by the

Khan's nephew, named Altan; then traveled five camels, laden with the tents and provisions of the twenty warriors of the entourage, and finally a group of six warriors formed the rear. All the men carried their rifles at the ready and sabers in their saddles, while each carried the classic Mongol spear in his right hand.

In order not to arouse anticipated resistance among eventual Baatar supporters who might appear along the way, the caravan appeared among the few Mongol herdsmen and villages and yurts scattered on the steppe like the entourage of a princess member of the Temük Khan family, who had lived abroad and now came to live with her relatives. The pretext for the trip was to introduce the newcomer to the lands of her tribe and its neighbors. The rest of the group, consisting of Jack, Taro, Ives, and Bodniev, were introduced as the lady's employees in her previous life out of the country. This was the prudent advice given by the members of the Council of Elders through their spokesperson.

The horses walked normally at a pace and only trotted in uninhabited areas, so as not to denote haste or anxiety, given the alibi chosen for the trip. When passing by the isolated yurts, the inhabitants of the same left their lodgings to greet the travelers, perhaps the only ones who passed by their houses in fifteen or more days; in this way, the trip had a festive tone. When the hour of midday arrived, the caravan stopped in front of one of the houses, and although the members prepared their own lunch, they celebrated with the inhabitants drinking a concoction prepared by them. The idea, suggested by Temük and his advisers, was to create a climate favorable to Orghana's cause by the time the true nature of the mission was revealed, and to prevent the villagers from turning in favor of the impostor Baatar in the event of a conflict.

When that night, while camping in the middle of the wind-blown steppe, Jack contacted Richardson in New York, he narrated the alternatives of the trip. The Englishman approved of the prudent way in which the mission was being carried out.

After another day of travel, at sunset one of the warriors in the escort approached Colonel Khulan with his horse and pointed to a distant glow on one of the far hills to the north of the road.

"They are looking at us with binoculars." The escort man reported.

Khulan nodded, then slowed his horse until he was next to the truck. Orghana opened the window she had closed to keep road dust out of the cabin of the vehicle, and Khulan told her.

"Someone is following us from the north. I don't know how many they are."

"Who do you think they could be?" Asked the lady.

"I can't know. If they are bandits, when they see the armed escort we have, they will desist from attacking us."

"And what if they are sentinels of Baatar?" Asked Ives, who was following the conversation.

"They will most likely follow us on our journey for a while, until they form an opinion on our purposes." Replied the Colonel.

"Will they talk to the villagers we have been with?" Asked Bodniev.

"Most likely they will." Answered Khulan.

"Then don't worry, as we have presented it as a formal visit from a distant relative." argued Ives.

"Anyone who shows up on the steppe is likely to be suspicious. In addition, Baatar will not like that a potential competitor appears who achieves popularity among the peasants who he considers to be his natural audience, especially if he detects that this competitor has a special charisma."

At that moment the head of the escort, Temük's nephew named Altan, approached on horseback. His men had already warned him that they were being watched.

"I am going to send one of my scouts to observe those who are spying on us." He said.

"That is, to spy on spies." added Jack.

"That's right. This man is my best scout. He knows how to make himself invisible even though he's just a few steps away. He and his horse glide over the rocks like the wind. "

In moments a veteran warrior appeared. Despite the intense cold of the afternoon, he was dressed in a light coat; he was riding a small horse without saddle; the man was armed only with a saber and the horse's hooves were wrapped in rags to avoid making noises when galloping on the steppe or walking among the stones. At a signal from Altan he galloped off into the hills where they had seen the gleam of binoculars.

Altan said.

"For now we are going to stay in this place and make a momentary camp, so that those who spy on us do not move either and my man has time to get behind them to get closer and determine their intentions."

Jack was meditating and Taro Suzuki asked him.

"What do you think?"

"I am thinking about the paradox of this situation. Intelligence, espionage and counterintelligence tasks in the middle of this desert. "

"These tasks are a constant in this part of Asia at all times. From the time of the English and Russian Empires and their competition in Hindustan, in the so-called Great Game, to the situations of conflict and rivalry between Russia and China, China and India, India and Pakistan, and many others, it has always been like this. Most of these spy missions took place and take place in deserts like the Gobi, in the highest mountains in the world in the Himalayas, and in desert steppes. They are often carried out by small groups of highly mobile men, as in our case. "

Episode 21

The scout sent by Altan to sneak behind the hills where men of unknown parentage had been sighted, a Kazakh named Türk, trotted his horse in a wide circle to the north, instead of heading straight for his target. The reason for this tactic was to avoid being seen by potentially hostile sentries, scurrying behind the low hills. Although in this maneuver he did not always have the presumed enemies in sight, his instinct and sense of direction guided him at all times.

When he estimated that he had already exceeded the position of his targets, he turned the reins of his horse and began to approach behind the suspects. Soon his senses, particularly his hearing, detected unmistakable signs of human presence; small sounds brought to him by the breeze blowing from the valley, as well as a whiff of burned wood from some fire the sentries had lit. Türk left his horse in a small hollow and continued the approach on foot. Altan had told the travelers that his explorer had "wings on his feet," and indeed, despite his age, the Kazakh would glide over the rocks in total stealth, without emitting any sound or moving any stone from his road. By peering behind a sharp rock, he was able to effectively distinguish sentries posted on the top of a hill lower than Türk's position at the time, so that he could see them from behind and above. In order to get closer he took extreme precautions and began to crawl on his belly to get to hear the conversations of the subjects. They were three Mongols, one of them older and two other young men. Located about a hundred paces away, Türk could see the four Mongol horses, that were trying to chew the hard grasses that grew in another small hollow similar to the one that the Kazakh himself had left his own horse. The sentries had built a small smokeless fire and were speaking very quietly in a Mongolian dialect. Other advantages of Türk to act as an explorer were his fine hearing and his command of all the languages and dialects that were spoken in that border of Mongolia.

It was already deep night when Altan approached the tents of the remaining travelers and quietly urged them to join him in a corner of the plain where they had camped. The fire that had been lit at nightfall was spreading for lack of combustible material and the area was almost completely in darkness.

"My scout is already returning from his mission." Altan explained.

Indeed, some figures came forward from the shadows, and the travelers recognized the man named Türk and his mount.

As a good inhabitant of Central Asia, the Kazakh first took care of his horse; he removed the rags that covered his hooves and brought him a bucket of water; while the animal drank he took out the simple mount that he had carried. He then approached the group of travelers.

Altan asked him in Mongolian dialect.

"Well, what have you seen and heard?

Türk began to speak as the Colonel translated his words to Jack, Taro, Ives, and Aman Bodniev.

"The three men are effectively sentinels for one of the tribes that follow Baatar. They have been placed in that position, at the exit of the valley inhabited by the Temük Khan´s tribe, precisely because they doubt the position that this chief will adopt with respect to the uprising of peoples that Baatar plans to carry out. From the way the sentries were speaking, it appears that they are planning to move shortly, when their leader returns from a trip to western Mongolia, and that they expect the rebellion to be very strong, with many nomadic tribes attached. By the way they spoke, they will sow terror in those who do not join their ranks. They are people determined to exercise violence."

A long silence followed Türk's words. The impact of the revelation was very strong, mainly for Orghana and Khulan. The scout continued speaking.

"They have sent a fourth man to the small town we were in before we got here. They seem to have an informant there. "

The travelers had all sat on tarps on the desert floor. Visibly upset Altan stood up and said.

"I will not allow information that endangers Princess Orghana and my people to reach Baatar."

He took his saber from inside his tent and walked away to the place where the horses were, asking Türk.

"I'm going to take your horse, prepare it to travel stealthily as you have done before."

The two men were lost in the shadows, and after a while the light footsteps of the scout's horse could be heard.

"What is Altan going to do?" Asked Ives Richart.

"I don't think you would like to know. Let him do. " Was Aman Bodniev's harsh response.

In the dark moonless night and with only the light of the stars that covered the Mongolian sky, Altan traveled in the opposite direction the path that had taken them from the last town to the site where the caravan was. He too had a highly developed sense of direction from his long journeys through the steppe in all kinds of climates and seasons of the year.

One thought dominated his mind. When Baatar's fourth sentinel returned from the village to meet with his companions and inform them of what he had learned from the villagers, Altan would intercept him and force him to speak. No one would ever know what happened to Baatar's henchman, his body and his horse would never be found.

That night the travelers could not rest. Learning that Baatar had spread his nets around them, and that he was planning to move the tribes shortly, was a terrifying thought. Guessing what Altan was about to do to prevent it was also cause for unease. Despite her bravery worthy of a warrior, Orghana was visibly upset. She too got up and as she passed by Ives Richart as she went to her tent she whispered to him.

"Follow me."

When they both entered the lady's tent, she began to undress and told her companion.

"Now, make love to me."

Episode 22

Altan released the pressure of his hands on the man's neck. The half-suffocated Mongolian horseman coughed several times before he could breathe normally. His terror was reflected in his eyes; he knew that his life was in the hands of his unknown enemy, who had knocked him off his horse out of the shadows, had squeezed his neck until he made him confess what he had learned in the village. Sure enough, Baatar's henchmen had an informant in the last village Orghana's caravan had passed through, and this informant had communicated to the rider his suspicions about the lady and her purposes. When Altan asked the prisoner if the informant had narrated his suspicions to someone else, the answer had been negative. Simply, no one had passed through the village since the travelers led by Khulan were there.

"Please don't kill me." Baatar's sentinel implored.

Altan considered the situation objectively. If he let the man go, he could go to warn his companions, who were the ones who had sent him, about the ambush he had suffered; it was a dangerous loose end. On the other hand, Temük Khan's nephew was reluctant to shed blood unnecessarily. He finally made a risky decision.

"Well, I'll let you go but you must leave Mongolia immediately. Those who are going to look for you from now on are your own companions. The best thing for you is that they believe you are dead. What I am going to do now they would never forgive you. "

Altan stood up, also loosening the pressure his knee was exerting on the rider's chest. He proceeded to disarm him and also take out the weapons from the horse, which was looking expectantly at the situation of his owner. The Mongol staggered to his feet, straddled his horse, and soon they were both lost in the shadows of the Asian desert on a moonless night.

Altan in turn mounted the horse he had led and headed toward the village. The horse's rag-lined hooves made no noise that might wake the villagers; the theme was outwitting the dogs. The imprisoned sentry had told him not only who Baatar's informant was, but the location of his yurt in the village. This time Altan knew that he could not be merciful. The informant who lived in the village outside Temük Khan's lands was a permanent danger to his people, and the only solution was to eliminate him, which in turn would serve as an example to other potential traitors.

In Orghana's roomy sleeping bag, the kisses and caresses had had their arousing effect. The lady whispered into her French lover's ear was what she now expected of him. Ives smiled and his head began to descend along the woman's torso, making her feel his warm breath on her skin. When he reached the level of her belly, it began to churn with excitement. The lady prepared herself to receive from her lover an experience she had always wanted.

The East Asian desert was home to strong feelings, and Mongolian women were known for their determination in seeking satisfaction in every way. Orghana in particular, because of her personality and her upbringing, knew very well what she wanted as far as love was concerned, and she had already decided that Ives Richart was the one to grant it to her.

The first light of dawn was beginning to illuminate the peaks of the eastern mountains when the sound of a horse's hooves was heard in the camp, muffled by the rags that covered them. Colonel Khulan, the only one awake after staying up all night, awaiting the outcome of Altan's task, widened his eyes to see the approaching shadows; just in case he drew his pistol from the holster and cocked it, but was soon reassured when he recognized the figures of Altan and his horse. The Colonel stood up and approached the newcomer, who was dismounting.

"Well, have you been able to fulfill your task?" He asked without further comment.

"Yes. They will no longer endanger the safety of our tribe. "

Khulan guessed what that answer implied, he asked no further questions and went to sleep, practically overcome by sleep. Prior to doing so, he woke Jack up to continue the nightly surveillance of the camp.

The next day, after a hot breakfast that would remove the cold of the steppe night from the body, Jack gave the order to leave for the caravan, organized as before, with a vanguard of horsemen led this time by Altan, then the motorized vehicle with the foreign travelers, followed by Orghana and Khulan on horseback, followed by camels with provisions and their drivers, and finally the rear of horsemen. The scout had anticipated to recognize the path ahead of them, as his role required.

After midmorning on the march, some medium-height rocky hills appeared in their path; the tops of the mountains were not covered by the grasses that cover the Asian steppe, and thus showed the mineral substrate.

Jack ordered the caravan to stop, so that he could climb to the top of the highest mountain and from there observe the surrounding plain, in particular looking for signs of armed contingents that might be associated with the followers of Baatar, or wandering nomadic tribes and their herds.

Jack, Taro, Khulan and Altan climbed the highest rocks, located about a hundred meters (330 feet) high, with a lot of effort at the highest part, quite steep. From there, and with their binoculars, they dedicated themselves to carefully examining the surrounding landscape. Indeed, at the southern edge of the field of vision they recognized a nomadic camp with what appeared to be a fairly large herd of cattle, a sign of an important tribe.

Orghana, too, wanted to climb the hills, to be able to contemplate from there the panorama of her country, Mongolia, which she did not know well. She asked Ives to accompany her on her climb, since the Frenchman was an expert in mountaineering and trekking in the mountains of Europe. Both carried pistols and daggers to face the eventual surprises that could arise in the wild environments that they were going to travel through.

Episode 23

After climbing the last cliffs, which required quite a bit of work, they reached the highest point of the mountain, and indeed of all the surrounding hills. When they appeared on the rock that marked the summit, the effort of the ascent was rewarded by the panorama that opened before their eyes. In a clear sky, the visibility was very great and encompassed a wide area of the Mongolian steppe and mountains. Fields covered with green grasses stretched for miles around, their monotony broken by small dots marking the locations of villages, isolated dwellings, and herds.

Orghana arrived first and was ecstatic contemplating the landscape. Ives arrived immediately and exhausted; he leaned in the foreground on the stone of the summit. The woman took his hand and drew him close.

"Look what a beauty! This is my Nation. " She said, her voice cracking with emotion, not lowering her eyes from the show in front of them.

The Frenchman wrapped his arm around the lady's waist, and brought his head close to hers, putting them into contact, which was possible because the woman was standing on a higher rock step. Thus they remained for a long time, while their retinas were filled with amplitude, sun, the blue of the sky and the light green of the infinite grass.

"You have good reason to be proud of your country." Said the man.

"That, coming from a Frenchman always so attentive to patriotism, is very flattering." Orghana replied, as she turned her body now facing not the panorama but directly her partner. She wrapped her arms around the man's neck and bringing her face closer, she kissed his lips; Ives squeezed the hand that encircled her waist, drawing her body toward his. The lady smiled and said.

"I want you to make love to me again."

"Here? Between these stones?"

"In front of this immense horizon; I have a reason to want it."

"What reason?"

"I want to get pregnant from you. Now and in this place."

"You know I can't guarantee that."

"But I also know you can try. Find a place to be the nest of our love." Taking the lady by the hand, Richart led her away from the top of the mountain and began to explore the nearby buildings. Suddenly he said.

"Oh! Check this out. What is this hole?"

"I do not know. It seems to be the entrance to some gallery."

Always with the lady holding his hand, the Frenchman entered what seemed effectively the entrance to a tunnel, undoubtedly produced by the erosion of the wind, rain and snow. From his belt he took down an electric lantern with which he illuminated the narrow passageway as he continued to enter. After about thirty steps he said.

"The floor of this cave is quite flat in this part, and mind you, there are dry herbs in abundance."

"How do you think they got there?" Asked Orghana.

"The wind has probably blown them from the meadow, or the birds have maybe brought them to make their nests. I have matches in my pocket. I am going to make a heap with these dried herbs and I am going to light a fire, to warm us."

"I like that, that my man builds a nest and gives it heat."

Ives began to unbutton his lady´s jacket and blouse, and they lay down next to each other in the heat of the flames.

The two lovers had fallen asleep. The first to wake up was Ives, who took his jacket and covered the woman's naked body with it. Without waking up, Orghana sighed as her lips formed a smile. The man went further into the cave to gather more dried herbs and pour them as fuel into the fire, which was consuming them rapidly. As he did so, his eyes made out what seemed to him a glow that briefly reflected the flames of the fire. Since he had not carried his lantern to examine the cause of the reflection, he gathered up the branches that he could and returned to the fire, noticing that the woman was waking up. The smile lingered on her lips.

"I'm glad you have nice thoughts." He said.

"It's that I think I am convinced that I achieved my purpose."

Ives Richart frowned questioningly.

"What do you mean? You mean getting pregnant. "

"Yes."

"How can you know?"

"Do not forget that I am an practitioner of Tengrism."

"What do you mean? Do you have powers ... are you a seer? "

"Yes... for certain things. For example these sort of things. " The woman, still naked, lifted her torso bringing her face closer to Ives's, and expressed softly.

"Now you have one more reason to take care of me."

"Which?"

"Your son."

Surprised to see how seriously Orghana took her own predictions about her pregnancy, Ives helped her quickly dress before the fire was completely extinguished and the cold outside the cave spread inside. As she did so, a fleeting memory came back to his mind.

"Ah! While you were sleeping I have walked a bit inside this place. It seems to me that it is the beginning of a cavern, although I don't know how deep it is... I think I have seen something in there... something like a glow. "

Hearing these words, the lady made a gesture that showed interest. She suddenly said .

"Lend me your flashlight, I'll see what's in there."

"I accompany you."

"No, you stay picking up our things off the ground and extinguishing what's left of the fire. It's already giving off a lot of smoke. "

The man was left to do his job, then sat at the entrance of the cave to wait for Orghana to appear, while shadows spread across the wide steppe. When Orghana returned to him, she looked thoughtful, although she remained silent.

"Well. You have seen something?" Asked Ives.

"We'll talk about that in another time." The elusive phrase surprised the Frenchman, but accustomed to the lady's ways, he changed the subject.

"We have to go back to the camp. We have been alone for several hours and no doubt the others will be asking for us. Let's take advantage of the last hours of light. "

Indeed, the shadows were already lengthening across the landscape when at last they saw the light of a great fire, and around it, the shadows of the vehicle, the recumbent camels and the men active in the tasks of preparing the dinner.

Colonel Khulan came out to meet the couple, visibly nervous.

"I was worried about you. Do not forget that we are close to the Baatar supporters. We were about to go out with Altan to look for you. " Orghana smiled at her subject.

"Don't worry, we were admiring the view."

After climbing the last cliffs, which required quite a bit of work, they reached the highest point of the mountain, and indeed of all the surrounding hills. When they appeared on the rock that marked the summit, the effort of the ascent was rewarded by the panorama that opened before their eyes. In a clear sky, the visibility was very great and encompassed a wide area of the Mongolian steppe and mountains. Fields covered with green grasses stretched for miles around, their monotony broken by small dots marking the locations of villages, isolated dwellings, and herds.

Orghana arrived first and was ecstatic contemplating the landscape. Ives arrived immediately and exhausted; he leaned in the foreground on the stone of the summit. The woman took his hand and drew him close.

"Look what a beauty! This is my Nation. " She said, her voice cracking with emotion, not lowering her eyes from the show in front of them.

The Frenchman wrapped his arm around the lady's waist, and brought his head close to hers, putting them into contact, which was possible because the woman was standing on a higher rock step. Thus they remained for a long time, while their retinas were filled with amplitude, sun, the blue of the sky and the light green of the infinite grass.

"You have good reason to be proud of your country." Said the man.

"That, coming from a Frenchman always so attentive to patriotism, is very flattering." Orghana replied, as she turned her body now facing not the panorama but directly her partner. She wrapped her arms around the man's neck and bringing her face closer, she kissed his lips; Ives squeezed the hand that encircled her waist, drawing her body toward his. The lady smiled and said.

"I want you to make love to me again."

"Here? Between these stones? "

"In front of this immense horizon; I have a reason to want it. "

"What reason?"

"I want to get pregnant from you. Now and in this place. "

"You know I can't guarantee that."

"But I also know you can try. Find a place to be the nest of our love. " Taking the lady by the hand, Richart led her away from the top of the mountain and began to explore the nearby buildings. Suddenly he said.

"Oh! Check this out. What is this hole? "

"I do not know. It seems to be the entrance to some gallery. "

Always with the lady holding his hand, the Frenchman entered what seemed effectively the entrance to a tunnel, undoubtedly produced by the erosion of the wind, rain and snow. From his belt he took down an electric lantern with which he illuminated the narrow passageway as he continued to enter. After about thirty steps he said.

"The floor of this cave is quite flat in this part, and mind you, there are dry herbs in abundance."

"How do you think they got there?" Asked Orghana.

"The wind has probably blown them from the meadow, or the birds have maybe brought them to make their nests. I have matches in my pocket. I am going to make a heap with these dried herbs and I am going to light a fire, to warm us. "

"I like that, that my man builds a nest and gives it heat."

Ives began to unbutton his lady´s jacket and blouse, and they lay down next to each other in the heat of the flames.

The two lovers had fallen asleep. The first to wake up was Ives, who took his jacket and covered the woman's naked body with it. Without waking up, Orghana sighed as her lips formed a smile. The man went further into the cave to gather more dried herbs and pour them as fuel into the fire, which was consuming them rapidly. As he did so, his eyes made out what seemed to him a glow that briefly reflected the flames of the fire. Since he had not carried his lantern to examine the cause of the reflection, he gathered up the branches that he could and returned to the fire, noticing that the woman was waking up. The smile lingered on her lips.

"I'm glad you have nice thoughts." He said.

"It's that I think I am convinced that I achieved my purpose."

Ives Richart frowned questioningly.

"What do you mean? You mean getting pregnant. "

"Yes."

"How can you know?"

"Do not forget that I am an practitioner of Tengrism."

"What do you mean? Do you have powers ... are you a seer? "

"Yes... for certain things. For example these sort of things. " The woman, still naked, lifted her torso bringing her face closer to Ives's, and expressed softly.

"Now you have one more reason to take care of me."

"Which?"

"Your son."

Surprised to see how seriously Orghana took her own predictions about her pregnancy, Ives helped her quickly dress before the fire was completely extinguished and the cold outside the cave spread inside. As she did so, a fleeting memory came back to his mind.

"Ah! While you were sleeping I have walked a bit inside this place. It seems to me that it is the beginning of a cavern, although I don't know how deep it is... I think I have seen something in there... something like a glow. "

Hearing these words, the lady made a gesture that showed interest. She suddenly said .

"Lend me your flashlight, I'll see what's in there."

"I accompany you."

"No, you stay picking up our things off the ground and extinguishing what's left of the fire. It's already giving off a lot of smoke. "

The man was left to do his job, then sat at the entrance of the cave to wait for Orghana to appear, while shadows spread across the wide steppe. When Orghana returned to him, she looked thoughtful, although she remained silent.

"Well. You have seen something?" Asked Ives.

"We'll talk about that in another time." The elusive phrase surprised the Frenchman, but accustomed to the lady's ways, he changed the subject.

"We have to go back to the camp. We have been alone for several hours and no doubt the others will be asking for us. Let's take advantage of the last hours of light. "

Indeed, the shadows were already lengthening across the landscape when at last they saw the light of a great fire, and around it, the shadows of the vehicle, the recumbent camels and the men active in the tasks of preparing the dinner.

Colonel Khulan came out to meet the couple, visibly nervous.

"I was worried about you. Do not forget that we have close to the Baatar supporters. We were about to go out with Altan to look for you.

" Orghana smiled at her subject.

"Don't worry, we were admiring the view."

Episode 24

Orghana had restless dreams that night. She thrashed about in her sleeping bag and muttered nonsensical single words, keeping worried Ives Richart, who slept in the same ten. When she finally woke up, the woman was covered in sweat, and said to her companion, who was looking at her confused.

"I have to return to that cave, I must explore it thoroughly."

"We don't know where it ends. It seemed very deep. "

"I feel like there is something inside it that I must discover. But my dreams and visions don't let me know what it is. "

Resigned, the man said.

"Well, in that case, I'm going with you... Do you smell? They are already preparing breakfast. Get up! Let's have breakfast and go to the foot of that hill. We can go there on horseback. "

They left their horses loose at the base of the mountain, letting them eat the herbs that grew there, and set out to scale the rugged slope again. At least they already knew the path that offered the least resistance to ascent. When they reached the cliff that was at the top, Orghana again stood there to admire the landscape that captivated her. While the areas to the west of the hill were still partially in shadows, from the east the Sun advanced in its upward race. Ives once again stood in front of the entrance to the cave, and put down the items he had brought, including some ropes that might be needed inside to tie up and unhook from any possible unevenness.

Unexpectedly the lady told him.

"Ives, dear. Excuse me but I feel that entering the cavern this time is something I must do alone. "

"I am not going to let you expose yourself alone to what may exist inside ... beasts, abysses or other dangers."

Orghana put a hand on his arm and insisted.

"I ask you not to oppose my wish. It's something I feel I should do by myself. "

Realizing that opposing to the woman's iron will was useless, Richart reluctantly gave up on his purpose. He gave the lady two electrical torches that he had carried, and a pistol with its holster.

"If you see yourself in danger, shoot. The echo will bring the sound to the entrance. "

Orghana stood on tiptoe, kissed the man's lips and prepared to walk deep into the tunnel, to what she felt was her destiny. Watching her depart into the unknown, Ives's heart clenched wishing he had accompanied her. However, he had to settle for standing guard at the entrance of the cavern, to avoid dangers from outside, since he did not know those from inside, which could come from the bowels of the mountain.

Orghana walked carefully, illuminating the side walls and ceiling of the tunnel, trying to register every detail in her memory. Some lateral branches opened on the sides of the central path, and the woman was photographing these alternatives and dictating to the recorder of her cell phone the decisions that she made in relation to the direction she was following. She soon noticed that the height of the corridor was increasing, due to the fact that the floor had a downward slope while the ceiling remained constant; also the width of the corridor increased very gradually, making walking more comfortable, as there was no need to bend over anywhere. There were no marks on the walls that could be suspected of having an unnatural origin; the only signs were evidently due to the erosion of water from outside as it flowed through the tunnel over millennia. Taking a deep breath to oxygenate her lungs due to the effort of walking, Orghana was suddenly aware that despite the distance already walked from the entrance, the air was still pure and did not have the characteristic smell of closed places; she wondered if there were some vents up ahead that brought the tunnel into contact with the outside of the mountain.

Meanwhile, at the entrance to the cave at the top of the mountain, Ives walked impatiently as time passed without news of the woman. To calm his nerves, he decided to go outside and return to the rock that marked the top of the mountain. Looking west, he noticed something moving and forced him to force his eyes. As he still could not determine what it was about, the man went to the place at the mouth of the cave where he had left several items that he had brought with him, and took some binoculars from their case. Returning to the top, he looked closely at the remote objects and was able to discern that they were dark spots moving slowly toward where the hill was. Ives tried to calculate the distance in miles, but due to lack of reference points he could not get a proper approximation. Although he did not know for what reason, the sight was disturbing, and he returned to the cave with concern. Did those points still far away represent a danger for Orghana, for Ives himself and for their companions? He wondered. The Frenchman fervently hoped the lady would end her visit and emerge again into the light, so that they could join the rest of the caravan waiting below.

At the main camp, Altan and Khulan were uneasy about the lack of tasks to perform. Finally Temük Khan's relative proposed to the Colonel.

"I'm going to ride the steppe to the west. Do you want to accompany me?"

Before the acceptance of the soldier, the two men, finally accompanied by the explorer departed carrying elements and provisions to spend the night in the open if necessary.

They rode, forcing their horses to gallop for a couple of hours across the infinite plain, finding no settlement or dwelling, no travelers or animals of any kind. The horses were happy to be able to run freely across the steppe. They finally stopped when the scout beckoned to them.

"What is it, Falid?"Asked Altan. In response, the man pointed them in a direction to the northwest, where they still couldn't see anything on the ground.

"What are you watching?" The Khan's nephew insisted.

"The birds. Something is scaring them. " The man replied, starting his horse towards a low hill, which was the highest point in the vicinity. The other two followed him, and on reaching the top, Khulan produced a powerful telescopic monocular telescope, which he deployed.

"Do you see something?" Asked Altan.

"Some very distant points." Answered the Colonel, handing him the binoculars. The young man also observed without being able to determine what it was, so he finally handed the monocular to the explorer. The man looked carefully. He then dismounted from his horse, crouched down, and placed one ear against the steppe ground. After a few moments he stood up, and with a worried gesture he said.

"They are coming in this direction. It is an army on the march. "

Episode 25

From a bend in the road on , Orghana noticed that the downward slope was steeper, and that the tunnel was penetrating more rapidly into the bowels of the mountain. Also the signs of water erosion were more evident, possibly because as it rolled down more quickly, the water pierced the stone with more intensity. Suddenly stalactites and stalagmites began to appear, those thin cones of material that hang from the ceiling of the caverns or rise from the ground, a product of the drops of water that fall from above on the cavernous floor, loaded with dissolved salts from the walls and roof. At the same time, the lady felt a gentle breeze blowing on her cheeks, the source of which she did not know. She wondered how the deeper the cave got, the more air circulated through it, and she supposed there should be some natural explanation further down the path.

The width of the tunnel grew steadily and the height of the ceiling above her head was also rising, but nothing had prepared her for what in the next turn of the road suddenly loomed before her eyes. A vast cavity in the rock, very wide and long, hidden by the shadows that her flashlight could not illuminate, extended in front of her feet, and most remarkably, it was covered by an underground lake, which stood in her way, forcing her to enter it if she wanted to continue her advance. Retracing her steps or staying in place was out of the question. Orghana felt an imperative urge to move on, whose origin she did not know, but some internal force told the lady that to achieve the purpose of her mission she could not ignore the drive. Shee took off her boots and hung them around her waist, rolled up the lower part of her pants, and put her feet in the ice water, trying to walk along the edges of the water mirror, noting with relief that the depth was not very deep on that side. It was elevated and she was able to advance unhindered, although the slope towards the center of the lake was very rapid and she guessed that it might exceed her height.

Orghana's determination was total and came from deep within her soul; she sensed that the fundamental reason for her trip was further down that road. After twenty minutes of crossing the still surface lagoon, and when she no longer felt her legs that were semi-frozen, the woman finally reached the opposite end of the lake. When she was able to get out of the water and sit on the dry surface of a rock, the woman wiped and energetically rubbed her feet, until she verified that blood was circulating through them again. Then she put on her boots enjoying the warmth that was still inside them, and continued her journey trying to walk as fast as possible to warm not only her legs but also her entire body. The lady ingested several nutrient tablets that she had brought with her, while taking a sip of water from her canteen. She never knew how far she had come down that path when a new wonder unfolded before her eyes.

A zenith light coming from some hidden hole in the ceiling was reflected in a thousand highlights from the sides, forming a rainbow by the play of light. Orghana's mind was slow to find the explanation for this phenomenon, until she finally understood that she was in front of a natural crystal palace.

Colonel Khulan, Altan, and the explorer Falid decided to hide behind some cliffs of a certain height, and wait for the rapidly approaching troop to pass through the site, since their road, according to their calculations, was just below their hiding place. They wanted to see the numbers, weapons and intentions carried by the men, according to the slogans they painted on their banners, which were reminiscent of those carried by the Mongol conquerors in the very distant times of the Golden Horde of Genghis Khan and his descendants, particularly the Kublai Khan. After waiting more than an hour, they heard the rumbling of the hooves of innumerable horses, which was amplified as they entered a kind of canyon between two high hills, on top of one of which were the observers. Looking in the direction the riders were advancing, Khulan first saw an immense cloud of dust raised by the horse's hooves, concealing what was coming beneath it. When a gust of wind temporarily lifted the dust, his eyes widened in surprise mixed with fear. The front of the line of horsemen was about twenty men wide, and the column stretched far beyond what the eye could see. The Colonel sat on the nearest rock and groaned.

"Heavens! there are many. "

Quickly recovering from the shock, the three men raised their heads just above the edge of the cliff, and set out to try to assess the large contingent beginning to pass in front of them.

Nervous at Orghana's delay in returning, Ives Richart finally made up his mind. He hid all the equipment that he had carried inside the mouth of the cave, took a pistol, a knife, two flashlights and a piece of rope, and prepared to enter the tunnel. Before he could do so, a muffled sound reached his ears that was undoubtedly produced by a large troop of horses, no doubt those he had come to glimpse from the top of the mountain.

Filled with apprehension at the noise and the lack of news from his woman, Ives stepped into the dark cavern.

AT THE CAMP THEY HAD set up the day before, Jack Berglund, Taro Suzuki, and Aman Bodniev, along with the rest of the men who Altan had led there, paced impatiently at the lack of news from their comrades who had gone out exploring many hours before.

Jack had finally made contact with William Richardson in New York. He unfortunately had to admit to himself that he could not answer the numerous and logical questions posed by the Englishman on the progress of the expedition. The man in New York City ended up saying.

"Jack, if the dangers increase and the situation threatens to spiral out of control, you should consider aborting the mission."

Episode 26

The visual effect produced by the reflection and subsequent scattering of light from a still invisible opening in the cave ceiling had a magical effect on Orghana's psyche, predisposing her to what was to follow. When striking a ray of light on the crystals formed and deposited by the saline contents of the water that filtered from above, it diffracted a spectrum of lights of all the colors of the rainbow from red to violet.

The woman marveled through the beams of lights, and when walking I the path, her body and her clothes were being covered in all colors with a beautiful iridescent sun. She walked more than a hundred steps until the overhead light was left behind, but already in her soul and her mind the passage from everyday reality to a heightened emotional state where all wonders were possible had occurred.

Without ever having consumed substances that had the effect of altering her psychic functions, the lady's nature and training as a Tengrist priestess made her a recipient of impulses that would go unnoticed by other human beings. She soon came to a crossroads, or rather a series of crossroads, at each of which the path in front of her divided into two or three branches indisputable to the eye of each other. Any wanderer lost in that labyrinth would soon lose all reference and, not only would he not know which of the ramifications to take, but he would also ignore how to retrace his steps if the chosen option was incorrect. But in Orghana's case, in her ecstatic state, such dilemmas did not exist. Invisible hands pushed her at every crossroads in the direction she knew to be the right one, though she couldn't explain why.

And then she suddenly found them ...

Behind the umpteenth curve of her the tunnel in front of her expanded high and wide, as had already happened in front of the underground lagoon, only this time the ground was perfectly dry.

On both sides of the path in front of her, two beams of natural light coming from the ceiling illuminated two very bulky static figures. Between them, the black tunnel opened onto the path beyond the place. Approaching one of the figures, the woman had to suppress an exclamation. In front of her stood what had been a large Mongolian warrior in life, seated on a kind of stone bench, still dressed in clothing of leather and cloth that time had partially weathered, with a metal helmet on his head with two natural bull horns on either side of the head. But what impressed the lady the most was to see that the helmet rested on the skull of the person who had owned it. She immediately realized that what contained the warrior's costume was actually a skeleton, that for some reason kept its shape without collapsing on the ground. In one of what had been his hands, the warrior wielded a long spear, and in the other one of the typical shields of Mongol horsemen.

Orghana moved toward the other warrior at the other end of the tunnel opening that continued into the depths of the mountain. The other figure was another warrior, identically attired and armed. The woman took a few steps back, so that she could look at the whole spectacle in perspective that was offered in front of her. This overview made it completely clear to her what she was witnessing. The two warriors seated on alert were the sentries guarding the passage and protecting what was at the bottom of the tunnel, whatever it was.

Orghana's heart filled with joy as she realized where she was. The object of her search, and in reality, the reason for all her efforts was in front of her.

Without further thought, Princess Orghana launched herself toward her destiny.

They had been watching the passage of the squadrons of horsemen for several minutes and were amazed at their number and armament; likewise, the legends on the banners left no doubt as to the warlike purposes of the riders. At a certain moment, a carriage appeared among the ranks of horsemen. It was drawn by eight horses and its exterior showed a certain luxury as well as an armor against possible attacks. The interior of the carriage was veiled by translucent fabric curtains, which prevented a view inside, but surely allowed its occupants to see from the inside out.

Khulan exclaimed.

"Undoubtedly, in that wagon travels Baaltar himself, guarded by his best men."

Altan stood up and looked at his scout who was sitting behind him.

"Falid, travel to our village and tell Chief Temük Khan what we are seeing. Tell him on my behalf that some three thousand soldiers on the warpath are possibly heading towards Ulan Bator and will necessarily pass close to our village. The banners carry legends of war vindicating Genghis Khan. Tell my uncle to gather all his troops and put himself in command. I estimate that the column we just saw will take about a day to reach the village. You must make your horse fly across the steppe and prevent anyone from seeing you. You must tell him that Baaltar himself travels in command of his troops, and that I believe a confrontation will be inevitable. Also tell him that we will be on our way as soon as Princess Orghana returns, who has gone out to explore the mountain. "

Falid slipped from the top of the mountain to the spot where he had left his horse, mounted it from a side and darted towards the town of Temük Khan to warn him of the danger to his tribe.

In the middle of the bowels of the mountain, Ives Richart heard the rumbling of the regiments that marched through the neighboring canyon. Since he had seen what was coming before, he had no doubt what it was, and although he had no idea of the size of the contingent, he could guess that it was numerous. The Frenchman wondered how the sound coming from outside was entering so deeply into the mountain, and as Orghana had previously presumed, he attributed it to possible vents that would be found in the tunnel ceiling, although they were not yet visible. All that made it more imperative to find Princess Orghana as soon as possible.

Episode 27

With great relief, Ives thought he saw a blur of movement at the bottom of the tunnel, as far as his flashlight could reach. He was standing between the two sentry figures guarding the entrance to the corridor, but out of a certain superstitious respect he had decided not to advance and allow Orghana to explore that part alone, which seemed the end of the road. Time would prove him right in preserving the woman's privacy at that stage.

Sure enough, some thirty paces away, a shadow was moving toward the entrance and toward Ives. He was soon able to guess the way the girl was walking and his heart filled with joy. For a moment he had feared that the depths of the mountain would never bring Orghana back safely. When the light illuminated the advancing figure, Ives could not contain himself and rushed into the tunnel and running came to the woman, whom he hugged tightly with tears in his eyes.

Orghana had a placid expression on her face and her lips wore a smile. She returned the kisses of her lover and stroked his head; seeing his tears she asked.

"Do you love me that much?"

Richart was back in control of her emotions, but instead of answering her question, he asked in return.

"How are you? Where have you been?"

Neither did the woman answer his questions, but she said with a neutral air.

"I'm fine." And then she added an intriguing comment.

"I've already done it."

Ives was about to ask her what she had meant by her last sentence, but his phrase sentence was interrupted by a great noise coming from one of the alleged holes in the roof that communicated with the outside of the mountain and renewed the air of the cavern.

Restless, Orghana asked.

"What is that noise? Is there a storm out there? "

Ives narrated the vision he had had from the top of the hill of a great movement of troops advancing across the steppe towards them. Orghana reflected on what she heard and added.

"I fear it is Baaltar who has already started mobilizing his troops. They are many?"

"I barely saw them from afar and a few hours ago. From the dust that their horses raised, it seems to me that they are very numerous. "

Although the Frenchman wanted to ask her a thousand questions about what she had found and about the meaning of the mysterious phrase about her finding, once again the lady took the initiative and said.

"Let's go to the entrance of the cave. I want to see with my own eyes the troops that are moving.

"But ... what do you think you can do against them?"

Ives's question was filled with bewilderment. Once again, Orghana's response was elusive. With a smile she said.

"You will see." Then she added.

"Where are our companions? Where are our horses? "

"They are surely waiting for you."

"Let's not waste time."

Just as Ives had had before, Khulan's reaction to Orghana's appearance was emotional. The Colonel dropped to one knee and kissed the lady's hand. The others looked with surprise at the degree of adherence of the tough military man to the lady.

"What do you know about this troop movement?" The woman asked watching the riders parade deep into the valley.

"They are commanded by Baaltar himself. He travels in a carriage guarded by elite soldiers. "Replied Khulan.

"How many men are there?" Asked Orghana again.

"No less than three thousand, all fully armed horsemen."

At that point, Altan decided to take part in the conversation.

"They are heading in the direction of Ulan Bator, and their banners are of war. On the way they will pass through our town. I already sent my scout to warn Temük Khan. I asked him to stand in front of all his men and await Baaltar's arrival. "

The tension in Altan's tone was evident.

Orghana thought for a moment. After having made up her mind she asked.

"Will we be able to reach the town of Temük Khan before these troops?"

"I do not think so. Maybe we can arrive at the same time. "

"Let's get going. There is no time to lose."

It had become obvious to everyone that Orghana had become the head of the group. Everyone accepted that leadership without wondering why. Only Ives Richart had a clue.

Indeed, an idea disturbed him.

"What has Orghana found at the bottom of the cavern that allows her to make decisions befitting a commander-in-chief of an army, and to be obeyed without argument?"

The scout named Falid had arrived at the village in a rush; he leaped from his exhausted horse and yelled to be greeted by Temük Khan.

The Khan was sitting in his yurt accompanied by the Begum, the chief of the tribe's Council of Elders, and the warlord in Altan's absence. They had heard Falid's confused explanation, the fruit of his excitement and fatigue, and then, with questions wisely formulated by the elder, they had finally obtained a picture of the situation and the approaching danger.

Finally, after pondering the situation, Temük consulted with his advisers.

"Do you think that Baaltar will stop to attack our town, or will he continue on his way to Ulan Bator, to storm the seat of the government of the republic?"

The military chief answered in a somber tone. "It is unlikely that he would move on leaving behind our powerful and well-trained potentially enemy army."

The head of the Council of Elders added in the same line of thought.

"Most likely, he will stand in front of us demanding that we join them and accept his leadership, and that we will eventually end up fighting alongside him against government forces."

"I will never betray my Nation." Temük Khan answered categorically.

"Baaltar must assume it, so he will approach on a war footing."

"We must then prepare to fight." Temük said, then, addressing the military chief, he added.

"Send a platoon of warriors to accompany all the women, children and the elderly to our fortress on the mountain for their protection. Then ask all the tributary tribes send their men and weapons to join us. We are going to form an iron shield in front of our village to confront Baaltar and his henchmen. "

An icy wind passed through the room of the yurt, before the certainty of a war that was approaching at the gallop of Baaltars horsemen.

Episode 28

The truck carrying Jack, Taro Suzuki, Alan Bodniev, Ives Richart and Khulan was at full speed on the flat, unobstructed steppe, while the riders led by Orghana and Altan galloped alongside, trying not to be left behind. All were urged to reach the village of the tribe led by Temük Khan in time to participate in the events that took place there. All were convinced that these events would be dramatic due to the power of the sides that would face each other and the fierceness in the fight that characterizes the Mongol warriors.

The morning passed full of tension for the travelers; the arrival of afternoon did not bring relief and they all knew that the night would not give rest to them, nor to the horses, so Altan and Khulan pondered the downsides of arriving on a battlefield with exhausted men and beasts.

The horn sounded in the village in the sky of the dawn of the new day. Temük Khan, who had not been able to sleep all night and had gone to bed dressed, limited himself to donning his battle suit, full of metal inserts to reduce the impact of projectiles and bladed weapons. The Begum watched him trying to hold back her tears.

As soon as the Khan had collected the weapons he was going to carry, the head of the Council of Elders appeared at the door of the yurt and without saying any other words, asked.

"What will you do now?"

"I've been pondering it all night. It makes no sense to expose all of our men in a slaughter against a superior army. It would bring the destruction of our tribe."

"Are you going to give up then?"

"No way. I've told you before."

"And then what will you do?"

"I am going to challenge Baaltar to a personal duel, only he and I will fight for control, and only one of us will be in command at the end of the duel."

"Sounds sensible to me, but you know that Baaltar is a very experienced and powerful warrior. He is also younger than you. "

"Heaven will dictate which of us he will overcome."

They both left the yurt. Obeying the sound of the horn, all the men came out of their houses armed to the teeth; they too had all been awake the night, and the tension was evident on all faces.

Temük had placed himself in the center of the long horizontal line of his horsemen, which was being nurtured by contingents arriving from neighboring towns. The spectacle was magnificent for the brilliance of the weapons and armor and the perfect order of the troops.

In the east the sun was beginning to rise above the horizon, illuminating the scene on the Mongolian steppe. After expectant moments, a movement that seemed like ants began to be seen on that horizon, and as time passed, the very long line of an army was outlined that was deployed, still very far, in front of the town, describing an enveloping circle. Seeing it, the Khan's men gulped nervously, they had never seen before so many troops assembled. The prospect of slaughter was clear to all of them.

Temük Khan waited in his saddle quietly. He had sent scout Falid up to the enemy lines, armed with a white flag. The Khan knew that they would let him pass until he reached Baaltar, that would think that he was coming to surrender on behalf of Temük. Instead Falid would challenge him to a man-to-man duel with Temük Khan. He discounted that the assailant could not deny himself in front of his people, especially relying on his own self-estimation as a combatant.

The Mongolian steppe morning would see a single man emerge from each side of the ranks of warring armies. The two rivals would gallop towards the nearby mountains and only one of them would return alive, bringing his enemy's severed head. Temük Khan eagerly awaited his scout's arrival with the answer that would decide not only his personal destiny but also that of his tribe. The warriors who obeyed him were also attentive to the return of their companion, and they guessed that on Baaltar's response would depend on whether many of them would see the sunrise again the next day, or would lie in the dust of the Mongolian steppe, with their bodies eaten by the crows of the desert. The restlessness of the riders was transferred to their horses, which impatiently thumped their kicks on the ground.

Falid returned and without dismounting from the horse approached the chief of the tribe.

"Great Khan. Baaltar accepts your challenge. The fight will be with the traditional weapons of the Golden Horde of Genghis Khan and his descendants. Firearms should be put aside. Both will ride up to the mountains accompanied by their Shaman, who will warn us when the fight begins with a touch of the horn. The armies of both sides must remain confronted where they are now. "

The Sun had already ascended to its highest position marking noon, the appointed time for the duel. The two enemy ranks had closed in until they were faced at a distance of about three hundred paces in a tense waiting prelude to combat.

From the ranks of his people emerged the magnificent figure of Temük Khan, clad in a red robe over which he wore an elaborate articulated gilt metal cuirass, which covered him from neck to legs and from shoulders to wrists. A metal helmet with a long feather covered his noble head, and in his saddle he carried his curved saber, a leather sheath filled with long iron-tipped arrows, while at his back he carried a long bow with a taut string.

Baaltar was also dressed in a green robe with gold embroidery, over which he wore a brown leather cuirass with innumerable metallic inlays, which covered his torso, neck and part of his arms. A fur-lined leather helmet covered his head and nape. His fat face had a sparse beard that covered his jaw and two long mustaches that hung on either side of his mouth, the gesture of which simulated a smile. In their midst the Shaman carried on his mount a long horn with which he would announce the commencement of combat. The two contenders looked into each other's eyes from about twenty paces, a tense calm prevailing throughout the plain.

The Shaman began chanting an ancient, barely audible mantra, recalling past struggles. At a certain moment the singing stopped, and the priest took the reins of his horse to

lead it towards the mountains where the combat would take place.

At that moment, a gentle breeze from the depths of the steppe brought to everyone's ears a roar that was still far away, but clearly approaching. The shaman, puzzled, frowned, annoyed that something trivial could interrupt his ceremony and the ensuing fight. Temük Khan stared away from his enemy and looked west, then saw a cloud of dust produced by horses, but at the same time his ears heard the noise of a vehicle engine. All those present, thousands of men armed to the teeth, fixed their eyes on the desert.

Episode 29

Seeing from afar the two long lines of men facing each other on the plain in front of the village, Orghana's heart shuddered. She suddenly feared that she was arriving too late to participate in the conflict and that the slaughter would begin at any moment. For this reason she spurred her horse to arrive as soon as possible and interpose herself between the opposing sides.

Altan and his men readied their firearms and sabers to take part in the battle, while in the truck everyone prepared their automatic weapons to fire immediately, as circumstances required.

A horseman from the village came to meet the approaching group, and in a loud voice to make himself heard, explained to Altan what was happening in the village.

"Temük Khan has challenged Baaltar to a duel between the two to settle the leadership of all the tribes."

Orghana heard the words of the warrior and without waiting for the others, she spurred the tired horse, making it go at full speed towards the center of the conflict.

When Temük Khan saw a lone rider speeding up to where he stood, face to face with Baaltar and the Shaman, he had an insight into what was happening.

"Oh no! ... this woman ..."

The defiant Baaltar smiled as he realized that the approaching rider was a woman on horseback, and screamed at his rival in a mocking tone.

"What's going on Temük? Now do you need a woman to come defend you?"

Like a waterspout Orghana passed with her horse through the ranks of Baaltar's men and stood before the three dueling men.

"Baaltar, you damned impostor. It´s me you must face. It is Genghis Khan himself who guides my steps and strengthens my arm. "

The aforementioned made a gesture of contempt and replied.

"You are crazy? What are you talking about? I don't fight women. "

Understanding that with her reasoning and arguments she was not going to be able to change the situation, the lady, in a movement of unusual speed, took her bow that hung behind her back and at the same time out a couple of arrows from the backpack. Before anyone could react, she proceeded to send two projectiles into the line of Baaltar's men, a hundred and fifty paces away. Two men fell heavily from their horses with an arrow through their hearts each.

A formidable hurray came from the line of the defenders of the village.

Completely confused, Baaltar only managed to say.

"Damn crazy woman. Do you want to confront me? Well, I'll indulge you and when I'm done with you, I'll kill Temük Khan as well. "

With that said, he spurred on his handsome black horse and sped off into the nearby mountains. Temük gestured to follow but the Shaman stopped him and said.

"Let them both fight, and save yourself for when Baaltar is done with this woman."

Orghana sped off with her horse in the footsteps of the impostor, and soon they both disappeared behind the first foothills of the mountains.

Faced with the unexpected course of events, thousands of men on both sides were left in a tense wait, the duration of which they could not foresee. Temük and the shaman remained in the middle of both rows of opponents, waiting for the events to unfold.

In the truck, Ives was seized with nerves because he could not help his lady at the moment when she needed him most. Khulan and Altan led the defenders of the village, in anticipation of what might happen.

The minutes turned into hours, destroying the nerves of all the participants, whose fate completely depended on the outcome of the confrontation between the defiant Baaltar and the heroine who had assumed the defense of her town.

The Begum stepped out of the yurt where she had stood and walked through the ranks of warriors to stand beside her husband's horse. He held out a hand that the lady grasped tightly, symbolizing her support.

The west sky was covered in orange and then red. To the east, the shadows that rapidly covered the Mongol steppe began to lengthen. The long wait represented an agony for all those present, who remained rigid on their horses or the infants on foot, waiting for the outcome.

Finally, a point began to descend from the mountains slowly heading into the field in front of the village. With the last lights still shining behind the peaks of the hills, the figure gradually grew larger, but due to the distance it was still impossible to distinguish who was approaching.

Suddenly, a collective exclamation rose from the throats of Baaltar's henchmen and reverberated like an echo across the plain. Temük looked at Khulan, who was watching the approaching figure with his powerful monocular telescope. With a sob the hardened military man said.

"It is a black horse. It is not Princess Orghana's horse. "

Temük Khan brought her gloved hand to his face, trying to hide his pain. However, the Begum beckoned to Scout Falid; He took the reins of his horse and sped towards the advancing shadow, followed by thousands of eyes. The envoy's gallop was very fast, but the minutes passed by filling those present with anguish. Everyone could see the two horses approaching in the distance, Falid's slim white colt and the black one that belonged to Baaltar.

Suddenly, the scout took the cap off his head, waving it in the air, and started back at full speed in the direction of the town. With a dim glimmer of hope Khulan trotted his horse toward the approaching shadows, one slowly and one quickly. He again raised the monocular telescope and observed the scene. His cry reached the thousands of ears that listened to him.

"It's Orghana! Only God knows why she comes on Baaltar's horse, but it is Orghana all right. "

That said, he galloped off towards the still distant figures. Ives got into the truck, engaged the ignition, and also sped off to the same destination.

No one fully understood what was happening, and all options were still open. As the minutes passed, despite the growing darkness, everyone could see that the rider who was approaching on the black horse was the heroine of the town. A new and formidable hurray ran over the plain, this time from the ranks of Temük Khan. Baaltar's followers lowered their heads, completely confused.

Indeed, Orghana finally entered the ranks of combatants and instead of going to Temük and her men rode up to the enemy ranks, who followed her march with regret. Suddenly, the woman pulled out something she was carrying dangling from her horse's saddle, and then threw it in front of the rebel warriors. The men at whose feet the object had fallen realized with horror that it was the head of their leader, contracted in the grotesque gesture, and still wearing the helmet he had worn.

The ranks of the tribes that Baaltar had commanded began to retreat towards the steppe from which they had come. The Shaman went towards the mountain in order to bury the defeated chief, and unite the head with his body.

Epilogue

William Richardson picked up the intercom phone, the call came from Lou, the man in charge of surveillance from the lobby of the building.

"Doctor, Madame Swarowska and Messrs. Corrado Gherardi and von Eichenberg are arriving."

"Please, show them in, Lou."

After cutting off the call, he addressed the members of the Bluthund Circle Executive Committee who were already in the spacious meeting room. Jerome Watkins, the Head of Ceremonies, was connecting the projection equipment, while Jack Berglund and Taro Suzuki brought chairs from other offices and arranged them in front of the desk from where the session was to be conducted. Richardson himself returned to his task of arranging glasses and the jug of water on the tables; he told his companions.

"The members of the European Committee are coming. Admiral Donnelly confirmed to me that he has already arrived from Washington and will be here shortly, so we can start the session. "

All the members had already greeted each other and distributed themselves to the chairs in the room. Watkins called the meeting open.

"Welcome everyone, we thank you for having traveled so far to attend our meeting. You will see that among those attending the launch session are missing the Mongolian lady, Orghana Ganbold and Mr. Ives Richart. The reasons for their absence will be explained in the course of this session. Now Dr Richardson will take the floor. "

The Englishman recalled with great conciseness the objectives of the Mission called "Tomb of Genghis Khan." Carried out by the Bluthund Circle, and then passed the floor to Jack Berglund and Taro Suzuki, who were responsible for it.

Both men explained everything that happened in the hazardous expedition, in which they had been close to being involved in a battle of great magnitude between two armies of Mongol warriors armed to the teeth, and the unexpected end of the duel between Princess Orghana and the Baaltar rebel. At one point during the presentation, Admiral Donnelly arrived, waving silently so as not to interrupt the speakers, and sat down in one of the free chairs.

At the conclusion of one phase of the presentation, Jerome Watkins asked the speakers.

"¿So Mrs. Ganbold, whom we believed to be part of the CIA, was actually a priestess of her religion and part of the Mongol aristocracy, as well as a fierce warrior?"

At Jack Berglund's affirmative answer, Admiral Donnelly added.

"We at the State Department knew that Madame Ganbold belongs to the nobility of her country, and that her mother is the High Priestess of her religion. However, we did not know what her true purposes were for going to her country of origin. "

"What is your Department's assessment of the mission's results." Richardson asked Donnelly.

"We are extremely pleased with the successful completion of the mission, and reassured by the fact that the threat posed by the rebel Baaltar to the peace of Central and East Asia has been neutralized. Big players in world politics like China and Russia coexist in the area, and what no one needed was a conflict to set that area on fire. "

The next question came from Nadia Swarowska.

"What is the status of Princess Orghana in her country today."

Jack replied.

"She is considered a heroine by most of the nomadic tribes, and as the representative of the Genghis Khan tradition. What's more, some think that the Great Khan's genes function embodied in her. "

"She hasn't been invited to come to this meeting?" insisted Swaroska.

"Of course, but it is a pending issue. Madame Ganbold, or actually now Madame Richart, is in the sixth month of her pregnancy. "

"So she has married our associate Ives Richart?"

"Yes. Both of them reside part of the time in Ulan Bator, and part of the time in the town of Temük Khan, who protected and supported us all the time. "

"In summary, can we say that all the objectives of the Mission" Tomb of Genghis Khan "have been accomplished?" Asked Corrado Gherardi. The answer came from Richardson.

"Yes, except of course the central objective of finding the tomb of the great Emperor."

Taro Suzuki, usually low-key and reserved in his expressions, this time exclaimed a bewildering phrase.

"I'm not sure that's true either."

And so, dear reader, this story has come to its end. But fear not, for new adventures await on the horizon, and the journey continues in the pages of tomorrow.

From the Author

D ear reader

    I appreciate your interest in reading these few words in which I talk about my work. It is a good habit to try to understand what led an author to write a particular book, because the motivations vary from author to author and from book to book.

As a sign of respect for the reader, in all my books I make a thorough previous investigation of the facts the work refers to, particularly considering that many of them take place in places sometimes very far apart from each other and also in various historical periods; my books often travel indeed through dilated stretches in time and space.

These searches are based on my memory, in the large family library and the huge quarry of facts and data existing in the Internet. In the global network everyone can search but not all find the same ... fortunately, since this results in a huge variability and diversity.

The plot of course comes from the imagination and fantasy. This is critical for me and I confess that I would never write a book that I wouldn't like to read; my interests as a writer and as a reader coincide to a large degree.

My works often take place in exotic locations and refer sometimes to surprising and even paradoxical facts, but never enter the realm of the fantastic and incredible. Moreover, the most bizarre events are often true.

About the Author

Cedric Daurio is the pen name an Argentine novelist uses for certain types of narrative, in general historical thrillers and novels of action and adventure.

The author practiced his profession as a chemical engineer until 2005 and began his literary career thereafter. He has lived in New York for years and now resides in Buenos Aires, his hometown. All his works are based on extensive research, his style is stripped, clear and direct, and he does not hesitate to tackle thorny issues.

C. Daurio writes in Spanish and all his books have been translated into English, they are available in print editions and as digital books.

Novels by Cedric Daurio

B lood Runes
      The Mystic warrior
  The Eagles Nest
  The Romanov Diadem
  The Knights templar are back
  The Mythical City
  The Lost Legion
  An African Adventure
  I Ching and Murder
  An Elegant Lady
  Bloody Equinox
  The Grail's Quest
  Whirlwind of Terror
  Game End in Venice
  The Bewitched Jungle

Contact the Author

Mailto: cedricdaurio@gmail.com
Blog: https://cedricdauriobooks.wordpress.com/blog/
Twitter: @CedricDaurio

About the Publisher

Oscar Luis Rigiroli publishes the books in print and electronic editions through a commercial network that provides them with an ample worldwide coverage including sales in the five continents. The catalog includes titles of its own authorship as those written by other authors. All works are available in Spanish and English.

Abundant information on these titles can be consulted in the following websites:

Https://narrativaoscarrigiroli.wordpress.com/

The reader is kindly invited to consult them in the certainty of finding good reading experiences.

ART Gallery

Milton Keynes UK
Ingram Content Group UK Ltd.
UKHW042003281024
450365UK00003B/121